LUTHER M. SILER

I0521531

THE
BENEVOLENCE
ARCHIVES
VOLUME 1

PROSTETNIC

PUBLICATIONS

This is a work of fiction. Any resemblance to real persons, living or dead, is coincidental.

THE BENEVOLENCE ARCHIVES, Vol. 1

ISBN-13: 978-0-9906253-9-1
ISBN-10: 0990625397

First Print Edition: July 2015

TABLE OF CONTENTS

FOREWORD

It all started with *Star Wars*.

Or, rather, it started with George Lucas selling *Star Wars*. The geek uproar was massive; if you're reading this, you probably remember. Betrayal, and terrible things happening to captive childhoods, and all that.

I stayed out of it, for the most part. I'll be a *Star Wars* fan until I die, and the idea that my two-year-old son's first movie in theaters could be a new *Star Wars* movie had more than a little appeal to it.

And then I read this interview with this guy. (This would be a better story if I remembered who the guy was. I've been racking my brain for a year. I have no idea, and my Google-fu is not strong enough to recover the interview.) Anyway, the guy was a writer-- comic books, specifically. And he was doing a promo interview for his new series. Which I can't remember the name of either.

Here's the part that stuck in my head: *Wouldn't it be great*, he said, *if instead of arguing about what George Lucas or Disney should do with Star Wars, we just took our inspiration from what they've already done and wrote our own stories?*

That's interesting, I thought, and went on with whatever I was doing.

But the idea stuck in my head. And a couple of days later, it was *What if Star Wars had been about Han and Chewie instead of Luke?* And a day or two after that, it was *What if Luke had just been a job, and Han hadn't come back at the Battle of Yavin?*

And a few days after that, Grond and Brazel were alive. Grond, actually, was an old D&D character that I'd been trying to stick into a story for years. Brazel sort of came out of nowhere. And then the first story, the one that became *Benevolence Archives 1*, was written-- the one I've called *The Planet it's Farthest From*, a reference that anyone familiar with the saga ought to recognize.

(I have just, at this exact second, realized that I'm writing this on May 4th, *Star Wars* Day. I swear that was not intentional.)

BA 1 starts with the line "I have a bad feeling about this." And there are scattered references here and there-- particularly in that first story-- that no *Star Wars* fan is going to miss. Be aware that I *want* you to see them; I'm going for homage here, not ripoff, and ... well, I'll let you decide whether I've hit my mark or not. The stories are numbered in the order they were written, which turns out to be more or less chronological. The exception, *BA 2*, is missing because *BA 2* is quite a bit bigger than the others. And also not finished. But I think-- and hope-- that the six stories you have here are going to be well worth your time. And believe me, there's more where they came from.

Thank you for reading.

Luther M. Siler
A wretched hive of scum and villainy, somewhere in Northern Indiana
May 4, 2014

(Print edition addendum: The writer is Brian K. Vaughan. The comic book series is SAGA. You should read it.)

"THE PLANET IT'S FARTHEST FROM"

I have a bad feeling about this, the gnome thought.

The saloon had a bad reputation, but precious little on this backwards shithole of a planet was thought of highly. The only thing that Kratuul was known to export was exotic fevers and several deep-space-capable varieties of mold; there was indigenous life that had been rumored to have reached sentience, but having met several of the locals he was unconvinced.

The saloon was located at the ass-end of a wide patch that had been hacked out of Kratuul's ubiquitous jungle. It was one of six in a tiny trading depot barely worth the name; the gnome couldn't think of a single thing he might want enough to travel to Kratuul in order to get it.

Well, one thing. It was inside the saloon. He'd have to go inside to get it.

I bet it smells terrible in there. Gnomes were blessed with an especially keen sense of smell, something that felt like less of an adaptation when it couldn't be turned off in malodorous places.   He smoothed his fur and adjusted his clothing, making sure his assortment of weapons were all in the right places-- easy enough to reach, less easy to detect in a quick pat-down-- and strode toward the door.

The door was rather bigger than he'd expected it to be.

Oh, hell, he thought. This was not a good sign.

He put his shoulder into the door, pushing it open slowly. The gnome was large for his species, but that still put him at barely over one and a quarter meters tall, even with the lifts he'd had installed in his boots. The door was clearly built for a species much larger than he was.

Always do your own research, you idiot, he thought. He hadn't been prepared for an ogre bar. *Someone* had failed to let him know that he was going to be looking for his target in an ogre bar. The only question was who to choose to blame.

The saloon, unsurprisingly, stank of ogre-- an odd mix of sweat, lubricant, and a spice the gnome had never managed to identify. It was surprisingly full; apparently it was happy hour, or whatever ogres called that. *Glower hour,* he thought, hating himself a little bit for the thought. The clientele was about what he'd expected: overheated, mostly male, sweaty, and mostly twice his size. Ogres were by far the largest of the recognized Galactic Types; they ranged from two meters at the small end to nearly three meters tall, and were generally as musclebound as they were oversized. Most of the patrons had legs thicker around than he was. And most of them were staring at him, scattered pairs of red eyes glowing in the darkened room. Several were openly laughing.

He looked around, giving his eyes a moment to adjust, and spotted an empty stool at the bar. The halfogre sitting next to the empty stool looked just as unfriendly as the others but was noticeably less massive than the rest of the clientele. He also hadn't turned around yet. *Stride*, he thought, and did his short-legged best to not look like he was waddling as he walked to the stool.

Which was taller than he was. He cursed under his breath. *Always do your own research.* He climbed up into the stool, which lifted him just high enough to see over the top of the bar-- which, surprisingly, gleamed; it was the one thing in the saloon that looked like it had any attention paid to keeping it clean. He cursed again and stood on the seat, pounding on the bar a few times to attract the barkeep's attention.

The barkeep did not appear to appreciate the gesture.

"We don't serve your kind here," he snarled. "I don't even have cups in goblin size. You see a kiddy table around here?"

"I'm a gnome," the gnome responded, sighing theatrically. "Not a goblin. Look at me. I'm wearing *clothes*."

"Unless they make you taller, I don't *fucking care*," the barkeep retorted, pulling his lips back and raising his voice a bit. His teeth were filed. "I ain't gonna repeat myself, neither."

"My money spends," the gnome said, trying not to notice that the saloon was getting noticeably quieter than it had been when he'd entered. "How about we start with me buying my friend here a drink?" He gestured toward the halfogre next to him, hoping that his neighbor was in a reasonable mood.

The halfogre pulled a knife from a sheath and slammed it into the bar, burying the tip of the blade three inches deep in the wood. *Not so much, then.*

"Why did you even bring that with you?" the gnome had time to squeak, and then all hell broke loose. The bartender, roaring, swung a bottle at the halfogre's head-- a bottle that was snatched from his hand and hurled across the saloon so quickly and easily that it almost looked practiced. The bottle struck a mirrored wall and shattered, spraying something foul-smelling and thick over a table of four sitting underneath it. Three of the four, all females, shrieked. The fourth, a male, who had been directly under where the bottle struck the wall, was completely drenched.

He stood up and tossed the table out of his way. The gnome took this in and then looked back at the bartender and his former seatmate, not sure which direction to bolt.

"Run," the bartender growled, settling the issue. The halfogre pushed his sleeves back, revealing arms covered in tattoos and a pair of wicked gladiator's gloves on his hands.

Right, then, the gnome thought. This was not going as he had expected. It had been a while since he had been in a bar fight. It had been longer since he'd been in one where the furniture was all bigger than he was. He leapt from his stool, hitting the floor hard and rolling underneath a table. The fight was already spreading, a pair of ogres having taken unkindly to having had a table thrown at them and a few others apparently joining in for the sheer joy of it.

A hand clamped down on his ankle. And most of his shin; it was a large hand. The gnome was dragged unceremoniously from underneath the table and shaken in the air. It was the seatmate, who *grinned* at him and hurled him bodily at the drink-soaked ogre across the saloon. The gnome flew through the air, hitting Wet Ogre in the chest and clinging for dear life to his clothes, digging his hands into the ogre's vest and holding on.

"Save me!" he shrieked. "I have money!" He climbed up Wet Ogre's chest, swinging himself over his head and clinging to him like a backpack. The other responded by whirling, trying to knock him off. He leapt instead, landing behind the bar and fleeing through a nearby door.

As it turned out, it smelled even *worse* in the kitchen, but at least it was empty. The sounds of combat intensified behind him, the first telltale whines of laser blasts joining the melee.

Window. It was higher than it should have been, of course, but at least it was open. The gnome leapt onto a countertop and from there to the window, clambering through and dropping to the ground outside, losing a few buttons off his shirt in the process. He fled, retreating to a darkened alleyway a few blocks away. In the distance, he heard sirens. The local constabulary was actually responding; surprising for a place like this. As fast as the saloon had dissolved into chaos, bar fights had to be a common occurrence. He waited, watching back toward the saloon, not willing to trust the open streets just yet. The planet was in unclaimed territory, far from gnomespace, and he was probably the only gnome in the settlement. It was likely that the constables would be looking for him soon, and probably not to see if he'd had medical attention.

A few more minutes of noisy chaos, and a shadow detached itself from the wall ahead of him. An uncomfortably large shadow. *No way.*

"Brazel."

The gnome breathed a sigh of relief. "Grond?"

"You should hope so," the halfogre said, shaking blood from one of his gladiator gloves. "Everybody else back there is busy blaming the fight on you. Did you get it?"

"*Did I get it?* Of course I got it," Brazel said, insulted. He held up a data chip. "I got the chip, his money, a shiv, and two different data pads to go with it. I'd have lifted his gun, too, if he hadn't spun around so fast. You care to explain why you didn't mention we were going to a *fucking ogre bar?*"

"Did I forget to mention that?" Grond said, sounding confused. "I can't imagine why. Sometimes I forget how short you are, you know. Was there something wrong with the plan?"

"Ass," Brazel retorted. "The plan was that you'd create a distraction and I'd lift the chip. In and out, easy. I was expecting you to *bump into him* or something, not to get chucked at him like a bloody throwing knife."

"Exciting, wasn't it?" Grond said, chuckling. "Can we go now, or do you want to yell at me for a bit longer?" He cocked his head, listening to the sirens, which were growing louder. "I bet I can convince the authorities I've captured you. We could charge more if we have to break you out of jail before we bring the chip back."

"I'm taking two thirds of the take," Brazel said. "It's the least I deserve for being used as a projectile." But Grond was right; it was time to get back to the ship. Revenge could come later.

"THE CLOSET"

"Found us something to do," the gnome said.

"Details," the halfogre responded, not bothering to look up from his book.   Brazel could be longwinded, and it was better to let him do the explaining than to ask questions.

"It's actually pretty straightforward," the gnome said. "Somebody owes Prescott some money.   He wants it back."

Grond waited. Brazel didn't add any details. "He happen to say how?"

"It's up to us, apparently," the gnome replied, grinning. "We can steal it back, convince the fellow to hand it over voluntarily, or just beat it out of him. Complete discretion.   I asked Rhundi how pissed Prescott seemed about it.   She said it sounded pretty routine."

It was never *routine* to owe Prescott money, Grond thought. Prescott handing off carte blanche on getting his money back to a couple of freelancers was a little bit on the unusual side, but they'd worked for him before. He'd normally have handled something like that himself; maybe it really just wasn't a big enough deal for him to bother.

"Here's the dossier," Brazel said, tossing a datapad in Grond's direction. Grond caught the thing one-handed, carefully setting his book aside and putting his reading glasses on top of it. The glasses were an affectation; he only wore them when he was reading something that was actually on paper. They helped pull him deeper into his reading, somehow.

The target's name was Arrakin Darl. The dossier listed an address in a rough neighborhood in a large city on a basic terrestrial planet relatively nearby, on the border zone between gnomish and dwarven territory. The pictures included were of a human male, 22 years old, of slight build. He looked like a junkie. Grond raised a scarred eyebrow at the amount he owed.

"How'd this kid get into Prescott for thirty thousand?" he asked. "He doesn't look like he's seen half that in his entire lifetime." Prescott was rich enough that he could have written off the debt with little trouble, but this amount of debt hardly seemed *routine*.

"No details," Brazel said. "I'd have told you already. For all I know he borrowed five and the rest is interest."

It would take about a day to get there, Grond considered. Maybe another two or three days to find the kid and scope the place out; another day to get back. Assuming there were no complications.

He didn't have anything he needed to do in the next five days.

"Usual rate?"

"Plus ten percent," Brazel said. "He's still being nice to us after the bullshit we got into last time."

Grond nodded, chuckling. Brazel had burned off a third of his fur the last time they'd done a job for Prescott. Their usual rate now included a grooming rider.

"Gimme an hour," he said. "I'll meet you at the dock."

Three days later, they'd found the kid and had had him under near-constant 'bot surveillance for a day and a half. Brazel had spent the time watching him while Grond and Rhundi checked every source they had for information about him. Other than owing unsavory people money, the kid was boring. He was a *student,* if you could believe that, spending most of his time commuting back and forth to class or in the library. The apartment was in a rougher part of town, but the kid seemed to live there mostly because the rents were cheap. Brazel and Grond hadn't seen him do a single thing that rated as dangerous, much less interesting, the entire time. The junkie look appeared to be just that; a look. The kid was just skinny.

"You'll be the scariest thing he's ever seen," Brazel said. "How do you want to handle this?"

"You stay with the ship," Grond said. "Stay nearby in case I end up throwing him out of a window or something; I may need you to catch him. The building's sized for bigs, so I'll go get the money. Or his head. I'll play it by ear."

"My ears, I hope," Brazel said. Grond's were mostly either scar tissue or missing.

"Joke away, pipsqueak," Grond growled. "Only one of us gets to be pretty."

Grond didn't pass a single person on the way into the apartment block and rode an empty hoverlift to the kid's place on the 114th floor. He wasn't home, which they knew; they'd watched him leave an hour before, and Brazel was keeping an eye on him. The first option was to toss his place and see if there was anything to steal, but Grond could tell seconds after breaking in that that wasn't going to be the case. The only thing in the apartment that looked expensive was a desk console that rivaled the one in Rhundi's office, but even for Grond something like that was too big to be portable. *The kid doesn't have much money,* Grond thought, *but he has priorities. He spends it on things he needs.* The fabber in the corner had come standard with the apartment, the furniture was secondhand. The desk console was handprint-locked. Hackable, certainly, but electronics were generally Brazel's thing. He certainly wasn't going to be able to convince the console that his hands were human.

He spent a few minutes rummaging through cabinets and the bedroom's one closet; no luck.

He almost missed the false door. It only took him a minute to pick the lock.

His eyes widened when he saw what was behind it.

He opened a comm channel to Brazel. "Braze, we gotta pull out of this. There's a—"

"Too late," Brazel said. "He just got home. Was about to tell you. He should be upstairs in a couple of minutes. Alone. What's wrong?"

Shit.

"Just be ready for me to need to go fast," Grond said.

The second the kid opened the door, Grond hit him in the head. The kid collapsed instantly, bouncing off a wall on the way down. *Huh*, Grond thought. He'd expected a fight. Instead, he'd knocked the kid out cold with a single punch. *Is he even still breathing?*

He was. Grond shrugged, tying him to a chair, stuffing a rag into his mouth and blindfolding him.

"Brazel."

"You sound less concerned than you did a few minutes ago," the gnome responded.

"Yeah, well… there's a full fuckin' suit of Benevolence armor hidden in a closet in the room. Four expensive-assed rifles, too. I figured the hardware was his. Looks like it isn't."

"Shit. He's dead, isn't he."

"Nah, but I hit him like I was hitting Benevolence, not like I was hitting a half-sized human with tissue paper for muscles. He'll be out for a few minutes. How do you wanna play this? The suit and the rifles are worth the debt right there."

"I wanna know where he got 'em, I think."

"So do I. Stay where you are. I'll wake him up once I'm sure there aren't any more surprises in the apartment somewhere. We missed something."

The kid was still out, so Grond took a harder look around the apartment, taking careful note of how thick the walls were and looking carefully for anything that might hide a secret compartment. He shoved the furniture around, checking underneath the bed and moving rugs. Nothing. The apartment's only secret seemed to be the hidden space in the closet, and Grond had that cleaned out in minutes, piling the suit of armor and the guns in front of the kid. *Anything else he's hiding is going to be software in the desk,* he thought.

"Braze, see if you can remotely hack into the desk console. Pull everything you can off it. We can steal it if we have to but getting it out of here is going to be hell."

"On it," the gnome answered. And then, a moment later: "You, uh, may want to turn the thing on."

Grond activated the desk's startup sequence. It displayed a hand outline on its surface, along with the text CONFIRM VOICE AND HAND MATCH. He didn't speak, waiting patiently for Brazel. It didn't take long before the display started flickering.

"Nothing other than standard security programs, Grond. Namey'll have the ice cracked in five. Go ahead and wake him up if you haven't already."

Grond glanced over at the kid, whose head slumped down as he turned around. *Awake already, and he had the sense to stay quiet. He's not an idiot.*

"Shake your head if you hear me, boy."

The kid's shoulders tightened up reflexively, then he shook his head.

Grond lowered his voice, speaking directly into the kid's ear. "In a second I'm going to take the blinders off of you and pull that rag out of your mouth. I need you to understand something, son: if I get the idea even for a second that you're lying to me or even *imagining* using a spell on me, I'm going to start solving that problem by ripping your jaw off. I know people who can get the information I need from you straight out of your living brain. The rest of you does not have to be attached. Shake your head if you understand me."

I didn't say piss yourself, Grond thought, as the kid shook his head, his pants darkening.

He walked back around in front of the kid again and took his blindfold off. The tears were already rolling down his cheeks, the bruise where Grond had hit him already livid and angry-looking.

Good. But we need a little bit more.

He didn't touch the rag in his mouth, leaning forward and staring directly into the kid's eyes. His eyes brightened, losing their usual dark brown color and brightening to a fiery, glowing red. Full ogres could do this with little effort. It had taken Grond months of practice.

"Look carefully. Think about what you've gotten yourself into."

Grond was dressed inconspicuously, wearing a heavy duster coat. When he'd entered the apartment building, he'd been wearing a hat. He stood up and shrugged the coat off.

Underneath, he wore his gladiator clothes: two bandoliers, crossed over his chest, both bristling with ammunition and bladed things of all descriptions. A breechclout. Well-used gladiator's gloves on both hands, bristling with spikes and blades. Next to nothing else.

Not that you could really tell. Grond's natural skin color was a pale yellow. Other than his hands and his head, though, virtually none of his original skin tone was even visible any longer. His entire torso, legs, and arms were covered in scar tissue and fantastically elaborate tattoos. Grond had spent his entire youth and a good chunk of his adult life enslaved and working as a pit fighter. The scars and tattoos were all trophies. Occasionally he'd thought about having his skin rejuvenated. He never did, precisely for moments like this.

The kid started screaming into the rag, absurdly trying to get away. The chair shook. He wasn't going anywhere, though.

One more thing.

Grond picked his bow up from the floor next to the kid's chair. Snapped his wrist, unlocking the limbs, the bow's energy string shimmering into existence.

"You know what this is?"

The kid sat still, his eyes wide, still crying. Didn't shake his head yes or no.

"This is an Iklis sniper's longbow. Her name's Angela. Say hello."

The kid didn't do anything.

Grond smiled, showing his front teeth.

"I said fucking SAY HELLO," he said, putting every ounce of bass he could muster into his voice and tripling the volume. The kid screamed again, making sounds that would probably be *hello* and quite possibly *please god no help me anyone* in the bargain.

"I can kill you with Angela from two klicks away with my eyes closed. If I have them open it'll be three. Go ahead and run around corners. I'll hit you anyway. That's what I can do *if*, somehow, you get out of the room. Which has me in between you and the exit. And you don't know how many of my buddies are out there, either. Ready for me to take the gag out?"

The kid nodded.

Grond pulled out the gag. The kid sobbed, gasping for air; it looked like he'd shoved it into his throat a little farther than he'd intended to. Or he'd sucked part of it into his airpipe, what with all the screaming and pleading he'd been doing.

"You owe someone I know a whole goddamn lot of money."

The kid blinked. "You work for Jarekh?"

Ha. "Prescott."

If anything, the name made him look even more panicked. "I paid Prescott back! I swear I did!"

"He doesn't think so. He thinks you're into him for thirty thousand."

"I only borrowed twelve!"

Hell, Brazel was right.

"Let's make this conversation shorter. I don't care how much you borrowed or why you borrowed it or whether you paid Prescott back already or who the hell this Jarekh is. I care that I got hired to get Prescott's money back from what looked like a spike junkie and instead I found a closet full of Benevolence hardware behind a *fucking fake wall.* Which you will now explain to me, so that I can decide whether I'm gonna kill you or not."

"B ... Benevolence? What?"

Grond moved out of the way, showing the kid the pile of armor and guns. He screamed again.

"It's not mine! None of it! I've never seen any of that shit before! Fuck, I gamble! I owe a couple of bookies some money! You think I'm stupid enough to fuck with the Benevolence? Are you crazy?"

Timed perfectly, straight into his ear, Brazel spoke up. *"Grond. I think he's telling the truth. There's nothing but sports schedules and research data on city planning on that console. The kid's in engineering school. We didn't miss anything when we looked at him. The hardware's a goddamned coincidence."*

"I don't like coincidences," Grond muttered.

He grabbed the chair the kid was tied to, lifted him three feet off the floor, and ripped the chair in half, tossing the wreckage into the corners of the room. The kid hit the floor hard, kicking feebly with his legs and screaming. Grond grabbed him by the face, lifting him back off the floor again.

"C'mere, you lucky asshole."

He dragged him across the apartment, shoving him into the false room in the back of his closet.

"You telling me you live here and you never knew about any of this?"

"I moved in a month ago! Fuck, I'm never even here! I spend all my time at school! Hell no, I've never seen this!"

He's telling the truth. Grond had never seen anybody so obviously scared shitless; he didn't have enough brainpower left to construct a lie.

"Count to a thousand," he told him. "You should be able to break out before you starve to death in there. I'm taking all your shit and giving it to Prescott. That'll get him off your back. Lemme make a suggestion: don't ever gamble again. I see you, I'm gonna kill you." Not waiting for an answer, he slammed the kid into the back of the hidden space and closed and locked both the doors.

"Pickup. Now," he said over the comm. "I'm tossing his couch out the window in thirty seconds. Meet me there with the cargo door open. I want to be outside the atmosphere in five minutes."

"Coming," Brazel said. "Rhundi will be so pleased when she finds out she gets to move Benevolence gear."

"We're keeping the difference, too," Grond said. "Think we ought to mention it to Prescott?"

"Yes," Brazel said. "He's adding twenty percent to our usual fee next time."

"YANK"

Getting yanked out of tunnelspace at velocity hurt. And it hurt uniquely; every cell of your body felt like it got shoved about a centimeter away from where it was, except no two cells went in the same direction, and it took a second for your body to convince itself that, yes, it was still all put together the right way, and nothing had fallen off, and perhaps the contents of your stomach should stay where they were, and didn't belong on the floor. Or in your lungs.

Getting yanked out of tunnelspace at velocity counted as one of Brazel's absolute least favorite things. Getting yanked out of tunnelspace at velocity to discover your happy little smuggler's boat surrounded by half-a-dozen Mal pirate skiffs and an obviously stolen Benevolence blockship was *worse*.

THEY'RE POWERING UP WEAPONS, the boat's AI said into Brazel's ear.

"No way," Brazel said. "I could never have guessed. I figured they just detunneled us to show off a new *paint job*. GROND!" Brazel was the *Nameless'* pilot; the cockpit wasn't really sized for bigs, although Grond had rigged up a copilot's chair in his quarters that would let him fly the ship virtually if he needed to. Mostly, though, it was used for the guns, so Brazel really needed his partner to be sitting in his chair right now.

"Already in position," the halfogre growled, and Brazel's viewscreen lit up with combat diagnostics. The blockship that had detunneled them was pulling back behind the skiffs; it would be lightly armed, if at all. Benevolence would have had the thing surrounded by twenty times the hardware that the pirates had. Brazel wondered how they had managed to steal it.

SHIELDS TO FULL, Namey squawked. BEGIN PRETARGETING?

"They're not shooting," Grond said. "Why aren't they shooting?"

RECEIVING A COMMUNICATION FROM THE BLOCKSHIP, Namey said. SHALL I TELL THEM TO FUCK OFF? I LOVE DOING THAT.

"Not when they outnumber us, dear," Brazel responded, making a mental note to speak with his partner about the personality he'd selected for the AI. "Gimme the holo."

A dwarven face shimmered into existence in front of Brazel. He figured it was probably female; it was usually hard to tell.

Wait. *No.* He knew this one, and it was definitely female.

"Shocksie," he said. "That was awfully rude of you."

"My name is *Shocks-the-Mountains*, Brazel, and you're under arrest," she said. "So's Grond. Let us board, or we'll blow you to bits."

"That is even ruder," Brazel responded, wrinkling his snout at her and signaling Grond to hold off on violence. "And last I checked, Mal pirates aren't government. Care to explain how I'm under arrest?"

She glared. Mal pirates weren't especially fond of being called that; the name was pejorative—they didn't actually call themselves the Malevolence; it was just a natural consequence of opposing a group that called themselves the Benevolence. "You're under arrest because we control this avenue of space right now and I say so. And I have six ships and you only have one. Stand down."

"Charges?" Brazel asked. *Any chance of outrunning them?* he subvocalized to the ship.

UNLIKELY, Namey spouted back in his ear. WE'RE FASTER THAN THEY ARE BUT THERE ARE SIX OF THEM AND THEY'LL BE SHOOTING. NOTHING TO HIDE BEHIND EXCEPT THE BLOCKSHIP. I WANNA FIGHT! LET'S FIGHT!

We're not fighting yet, he subvoced.

"Quit chirping to your ship," Shocks-the-Mountains boomed over the holo channel. "Kidnapping. Theft. Murder.   Destruction of property. Shall I continue?"

"KIDNAPPING?" Grond roared. He wasn't on the holo channel; Brazel figured Shocksie probably heard him anyway.

"It's not kidnapping if the client is the person you're kidnapping. The word for that is *rescue*," Brazel corrected.

"It's kidnapping if it's my *son*, you wretch," the enraged dwarf bellowed back. "No dwarven male of my line gets to *ask* for rescue. He is *mine*."

Dwarven society was highly matriarchal. Brazel chose not to press the topic any longer, slowly backing the *Nameless* away from the skiffs.

"Well, I don't feel like being arrested today," Brazel said, "and Namey would be awfully upset if you dismantled him. So if you don't mind, turn off the blockship and I'll just—"

Laser fire erupted from four of the six skiffs and the *Nameless* at the same time. Flashes from the shields popped, darkening the viewscreen and forcing Brazel to navigate by the display. He threw the ship into a spin and accelerated directly toward the blockship.

"Is that a good idea?" Grond said over the comm.

"It makes 'em pay for it if they miss," Brazel said. "Namey, the thing's shielded, right?"

QUITE, the AI replied.

"Well, it makes 'em pay for it a little, then," he said, swooping around the ship. One of the skiffs disappeared off his viewscreen, replaced with a cartoony X.

"Got one," Grond said.

"Start using explosives, chaff, whatever we've got," Brazel said, partly talking to the AI and partly to Grond. He was struggling to remember the last time he'd had to upgrade the ship's armory; the *Nameless* wasn't exactly built for extended combat operations. The shields were upgraded to hell—and a near miss from *something* boomy rocked him in his seat, making him freshly pleased with that fact—but they didn't have much that was going to get through the shielding that blockship probably had.

Another skiff blinked off the viewscreen. Grond chortled over the comm.

There were four skiffs left, and they were doing their best to keep the *Nameless* surrounded, with his ship in between them and the blockship. Brazel picked one at random, highlighting it on the viewscreen, still doing his damnedest to dodge laser fire.

"Grond. I'm heading straight for—"

The ship went spinning as a massive explosion overtook their shields and tossed them away from the blockship. *What in the—*

BLOCKSHIP DESTROYED. TUNNELSPACE IS AVAILABLE AGAIN.

"Grond, did you do that?"

"I didn't," the halfogre said. "Did you?"

BENEVOLENCE FORCES DETECTED. RECOMMEND SPEEDY EXIT.

Oh, shit. The Benevolence had detected the tunnel pull somehow. And they'd found their missing ship that quickly.

"Go," Brazel told the AI. "Somewhere. Anywhere. Go go go go *now.*" His viewscreen was starting to fill up with Benevolence ID codes, what looked like an entire *fleet* of ships.

THIS IS IMPRESSIVELY BAD LUCK, Namey said.   IT APPEARS THAT THE BLOCKSHIP MANAGED TO PULL A BENEVOLENCE SHIP OUT OF TUNNELSPACE BY ACCIDENT. THE REST OF THEM FOLLOWED.

"So fucking *take advantage!*" Brazel said. "Get us the hell out of here before they notice us." The Benevolence spiderships had already blown two of the four skiffs into flaming powder. The other two were fleeing in opposite directions. No one was after them yet.

THEY'RE SCANNING FOR ID CODES. YOU WANT ME TO LIE, RIGHT?

"Yes!" Brazel said, hoping that his own ship was screwing with him, and punched the ship into tunnelspace, hoping the Benevolence didn't have another blockship with them.   The *Nameless* shuddered a bit and jumped, his viewscreen fading to black.

"That was close," Grond said.

"Poor Shocksie," Brazel said. "I kinda liked her. Should we tell Walks-the-Waves what happened?"

"Maybe leave the part where she was shooting at us out of it?"

"I think so," Brazel said. And after that, he would work on how the Mals had managed to get ahold of a blockship. That sounded like something that Rhundi would want to know. *Nothing's ever easy,* he thought to himself.

-{⊡}-

"REMEMBER"

They were halfway home from a successful job when the message came through.

Well, not a message, precisely. A set of coordinates, a timestamp, and a single word. The timestamp was two standard days away. So were the coordinates. The word was REMEMBER.

"Grond," Brazel said over the shipwide comm. "You may wanna come look at this."

A moment later, the halfogre was there, leaning forward into the cockpit, which was much too small for him. "What? I was reading."

"That," Brazel said, pointing at the screen.

He heard Grond mumble something under his breath.

"You know anything about this?" the gnome asked. "That's in the Queris system. Hell if I've ever even *been* to the Queris system. I certainly don't remember pissing anyone off there."

"I've been there," Grond said. "But not for a very long time." He stared at the coordinates. "Pull up a map. Let's see this a little closer up."

Brazel manipulated the map. The coordinates were ... nowhere. The Queris system was four planets, around an utterly average-looking star; the one named planet was nearly exactly opposite in its orbit from where they were being sent. There was nowhere terrestrial, much less inhabited, anywhere near it.

"And I suppose that two days from now there isn't going to be anything there either," Brazel said. "There's no way Queris orbits that fast, is there?"

"It doesn't," Grond muttered. "Remember. There's ... ah, *shit.*"

"We're going to die, aren't we," the gnome said. "How's it going to happen?"

The halfogre chuckled. "*Remember.* It's not a suggestion, Brazel. We're idiots. It's a fucking *name.* Lady Remember's called us. It's a *job.*"

Several expressions-- annoyance, surprise, shame, and more than a touch of fear-- crawled across Brazel's face all at once.

"*The* Remember?" Brazel spluttered, his fur involuntarily standing up. "*That* Remember? Remember needs something from *us?* When did we get so important?"

"Oh, we aren't. We're still going to die," Grond rumbled. "She probably just needs someone for a suicide mission. Or cannon fodder of some kind. I'm still guessing we're not about to ignore Remember asking us to drop by."

"We are not," Brazel said. "Not on this life am I gonna ignore Remember telling me to do something.

You wanna comm Rhundi and let her know that we're not coming straight back?"

The halfogre grinned. "How come I have to do it? You're about to miss something, aren't you?"

"Birthdays," the gnome grunted. "Three of 'em, in the same week. I don't know how--"

"Yes, you do," Grond corrected. "Think about when *your* birthday is."

"Shut up and make the call," Brazel said. "We've got just enough fuel to get to her. I hope there's a supply cache we can raid somewhere before we do whatever she's calling us about."

"I suspect she does," the halfogre replied, heading to his quarters to comm Brazel's wife.

No one was quite sure what Remember was.

She had an elf's lifespan, or she'd figured out how to magic her way into it. Just the stories Brazel had heard about her were too much for one regular-breed human to have accomplished, and there were doubtless plenty that Brazel had never heard. He could remember his parents and grandparents telling him stories about Remember, too; to the class of people likely to end up as a smuggler, the way Brazel had, the woman was a combination of a living legend and a demon.

It was Remember's job to know things. There were any number of organizations, both legit and otherwise, that would have gleefully sacrificed the population of entire planets in order to gain access to her sea of contacts and informers. People went to Remember—

sometimes paying large sums of money to dishonest "friends" of hers to arrange a meeting— when they needed to know things.   Sometimes she required payment. Sometimes she refused it. On rare occasions, she would summon people to her or-- more rarely-- seek someone out in order to pass on a piece of information. Her motivations for doing so were rarely clear. Some people insisted that she didn't ever *have* reasons-- that she'd just set things in motion on a lark. Brazel was sure she was playing some sort of long game. It just wasn't clear what.

And she wanted Brazel and his partner for a job.

The coordinates in the Queris system were nearly exactly two days of tunnelspace away-- which was a bit alarming.   It implied that Remember not only knew how to directly comm the *Nameless*, she knew its *exact location* when she did, and had timed the meeting to ensure that Brazel and Grond came directly to her-- no time to get back home for a refuel and resupply or, critically, to pick up any passengers or extra muscle. Not that they often needed extra muscle with a halfogre on board, but still. If nothing else, Rhundi had proven herself to be more than capable in a firefight-- possibly more capable than Brazel, who preferred to talk his way out of trouble rather than fight.

Of course, Brazel didn't *know* that Remember wanted them for a job.   It was possible that they'd crossed her somehow and she was bringing them in to have them killed. That felt like Remember's style; there was no reason to hire expensive thugs to hunt the two of them down when she could just summon them to their own deaths and have them pay for their own fuel.

There was little else to do on the way to the meet other than discuss Remember's motives, and since they didn't have any real idea what those were, Brazel and Grond spent most of the trip arguing. Rhundi was no help; she wasn't foolish enough to suggest that the two insult Remember but in her mind that was no reason to be nice about it.

"I've got thirteen kids," Brazel said, after attending the birthday party of his fourth-youngest via comm. "I don't need this shit."

"Fourteen," Grond corrected.

"Whatever," the gnome groused. "This had better be worth it."

It surprised neither of them that when they reached the rendezvous point there was nothing there. Remember would almost certainly have some sort of remote or 'bot in the area scanning for their ship; they were going to wait for her, not the other way around-- although Brazel was certain that their punctuality was still expected.

"Scan ... hell, scan everything," Brazel told the ship. "If there's anything out there bigger than two carbon molecules jammed together, I want to know about it."

MY SENSORS DO NOT OPERATE AT THAT RESOLUTION, Namey responded.   ALSO THAT WOULD BE TERRIBLY BORING.

"One of these days I'm reprogramming you into something subservient," the gnome grumbled. This was unlikely; the ship had been a lippy bastard for as long as he'd owned it and he had made that threat any number of times.

NOTHING WITHIN RANGE AT ALL, the ship blipped. NO RESIDUAL ENERGY SIGNATURES, EITHER. THERE HAS BEEN NO SHIP OR PROBE HERE WITHIN THE PAST THREE STANDARD DAYS.

Right about then was when the proximity alarms started.

The ship-- no, it was too big for a ship, the *moon*-- filled the viewscreen entirely, and appeared to be no more than a few klicks away from the *Nameless*. If it hadn't popped into view they'd have plowed into it in seconds. As it was, Brazel had to nearly tear the yoke off to pull the ship back, running parallel with the ... with *whatever the hell it was* instead of directly toward it.

"The shit is that?" Grond said over the ship's comm. The halfogre was in place in his copilot's chair in his quarters; he had access to a projected view of Brazel's viewscreen. "Is that a *ship?*"

Namey had lost his smugness all the sudden. THE OBJECT IS FOUR KILOMETERS IN DIAMETER, he said. IT DID NOT JUST EXIT TUNNELSPACE. IT WAS ALREADY THERE. IT APPEARS TO BE ENTIRELY ARTIFICIAL IN NATURE.

"Hail it," Brazel commanded.

THOUGHT OF THAT ALREADY, the ship responded. NO RESPONSE. THERE APPEARS TO BE A DOCKING PORT ON THE OBJECT'S FAR SIDE. NO SIGN OF SHIELDS OR WEAPONS POWERING UP.

"There was no sign of the *entire goddamn thing* two minutes ago," Brazel said. "I don't trust your sensors anymore."

WE HAVE NOT BEEN DESTROYED. I DO NOT BELIEVE MY SHIELDS WOULD HOLD UP LONG AGAINST ANY WEAPON SYSTEMS THAT OBJECT POSSESSES.

"Ship's right," Grond said. "Let's go take a look at that port."

It took only a few minutes to circle the object. It showed no sign of life; no ships emerged from it and no apparent weapon or scanning systems tracked them as they flew around it. The docking port was big enough to fly a capital ship through and was unshielded.

"Scan it for everything," Brazel said again.

THE OBJECT IS MOSTLY HOLLOW, Namey reported. AND THERE IS SOMETHING INSIDE THAT IS EITHER GENERATING OR UTILIZING AN ENORMOUS AMOUNT OF POWER. WE HAVE NOT BEEN HAILED AND I HAVE BEEN PROVIDED WITH NO SCHEMATICS. WE ARE FLYING BLIND.

"That's Remember for ya," Grond said. "She's screwing with us."

"I'd think I'd have *heard about it* if she lived in a spaceship the size of a small moon, though, wouldn't you?"

"One would think," Grond agreed. "Maybe it's new?"

"And required an entire shipyard for two years, plus the GDP of an entire planetary system to build?" Brazel asked. But there was no denying the object; it was too big to be a hologram and, besides, had fooled Namey. The thing was real. "Is this fucker that rich?"

"I suggest we find out," Grond said. "Perhaps she shares."

"Screw it," Brazel said. "In we go."

He activated the ship's external lights as well as all its sensors and flew in through the docking port. The port itself opened into what was effectively a smooth corridor, if an absurdly big one; the floor looked flat enough to land Namey virtually anywhere but Brazel decided to continue on until he spotted something that looked more like a designated landing area. There were no other ships and nothing moving, living or artificial.

The corridor continued until they'd penetrated about a kilometer into the station, at which point the walls fell away to emptiness and the floor continued on underneath them, a gangway now instead of a corridor, continuing into the center of the object. Namey's external lights were no longer sufficient to penetrate into the darkness; the hollow area was simply too big.

"Namey, get me a map," Brazel asked the ship, and then the lights came on, and the entire interior of the object blazed into view.

There wasn't much to see.

They were in the inside of the sphere, and the walls fell away on either side of them and curved back together at the other end, just over two kilometers away. The place clearly had gravity of some sort; there was a landing pad able to accommodate a ship three times the *Nameless'* size just ahead of them, and then a narrow walkway— perhaps wide enough for four or

five bigs to walk abreast, or seven or eight gnomes—
that led to a structure in the center of the sphere. The
structure was supported by a spire, with thick cabling
coming off it in every direction heading out to various
points on the inside of the sphere.

"What am I looking at, boat?" Brazel asked.

UNCLEAR, Namey responded.   BUT THE
OBJECT APPEARS TO BE BEGINNING TO
POWER ITSELF UP.   READING ENERGY
DISCHARGES THROUGHOUT THE STRUCTURE.
WHATEVER IS IN THE CENTER OF THE SPHERE
REQUIRES AN ASTONISHING AMOUNT OF
POWER.

"Sounds dandy. Land," the gnome ordered. "Grond,
suit up. Grab everything you own that can be used to
break something. Let's go see what's in there. Namey,
is there—"

THE SPHERE IS ESTABLISHING AN
ATMOSPHERE, AND THE DOCKING PORT HAS
CLOSED, the ship responded.   INTERIOR
TEMPERATURE IS CLIMBING. I PROJECT THAT
THE INTERIOR WILL BE SURVIVABLE IN TEN
MINUTES AND COMFORTABLE IN THIRTY.

"Let's be ready in fifteen," Brazel said, heading off
to his quarters to change. If he was going to be meeting
Lady Remember, he was certainly going to do it in
nicer clothes.

Grond was armed and ready in five minutes; it took
Brazel twenty, as the gnome rejected three different
outfits before settling on something that was an

acceptable mix of stylish enough to meet with one of the galaxy's most powerful people and utilitarian enough to be able to conceal a number of small weapons and useful tools underneath. The gnome suspected he would be searched; he had several items that he assumed or hoped would be found and a few, more carefully hidden, that even a scan ought not to locate. The halfogre was not dressed for subtlety at all; he wore his gladiator's gear: two bandoliers, weighted down with ammunition and weaponry, crossed over his chest; spiked gloves on his hands, and minimalistic protective gauntlets on his forearms and greaves on his calves. His Iklis sniper's longbow, lovingly named Angela, was slung over his back, and two heavy guns hung at his waist. The only other thing he was wearing was a multicolored, ragged-edged thermal uticloak; the thing looked a horror to Brazel, but it provided a few dozen places to hide additional useful sharp things and could even produce its own heat for low-temperature environments. He'd found the time to treat his skin with something, too; his tattoos glittered in the low light of the *Nameless'* cargo hold.

"Good day to die?" Grond asked. The gnome nodded once, grinning, and they exited the ship into the sphere.

Nothing happened as they followed the walkway to the structure in the center of the sphere. There was a low electrical hum, almost too low for Brazel's ears to pick it up, as the machinery of the sphere continued to power up, and a slight breeze from the newly created atmosphere tickled his fur. The gnome stayed directly in the center of the walkway; the manufacturers had neglected to include guardrails on either side and he wanted room to roll if he needed to without falling off. Grond paced him, following a few steps behind, not quite openly carrying weaponry yet but clearly itching to.

The structure ahead was dome-shaped, perhaps ten meters high in the center, with a single door and no windows anywhere. It was the same steel-grey color that the rest of the sphere was. *There hasn't been a single word or direction or sign written anywhere on this thing*, Brazel thought. No decoration or ornamentation or even any color anywhere. It had to have cost more money than Brazel and Grond would clear in several lifetimes to build the thing; the owner hadn't bothered to invest in *paint*. Strange.

The doorway noiselessly slid open as the pair approached. The space inside was dark.

"We going in there?" Brazel asked.

"I imagine we are," Grond replied. "Otherwise you got all dressed up for nothin'." The ogre muttered something Brazel couldn't hear, subvocalizing a command to the ship. "Namey says that he's figured out at least a little bit of what's going on around here, but he doesn't like it. The entire damn place is a power plant. And everything it's generating is getting funneled into this room. Whatever's in there is pulling enough energy to run a mid-sized city for a month."

Brazel tried to run the credits in his head again and gave up.

"Also, there's a scanner just inside the door," Grond said.

Brazel shrugged. "Not like she doesn't know we're here," he said, and walked inside. He actually *felt* the body scan; his fur rippled and he felt prickles on his skin even through the layers of fur and clothes on top of it. Remember wasn't bothering to be subtle; she wanted them to know this was happening. The lights came on.

The room was empty. It was also much smaller on the inside than it looked from outside-- the dome had been maybe ten meters high, but the interior space was a rounded cube perhaps four or five meters to a side. Other than the doorway, Brazel couldn't see a mark or a seam anywhere. The ceiling, walls and floor were covered in some sort of material he didn't recognize; a black matte color, textured like very soft rubber, spongy to the touch.

As soon as Grond stepped inside, the door slid closed behind him. As Brazel watched, the black material flowed over the doorway. Five seconds later the way out was all but invisible.

"I have a bad feeling about this," Grond said. The halfogre stood perfectly still, hands on his guns, waiting for something to happen.

A moment later *everything* happened. Brazel felt, rather than heard, the immense energies the sphere was generating slamming into the dome they were standing in, and a sound like a sun exploding assaulted his ears, the vibration going straight into his bones. He felt movement, and the material on the walls abruptly expanded, trapping him inside, immobile, blind, and suddenly blessedly deaf.

Everything went away.

>{ꙮ}<

Brazel awoke on the floor, some time later, his head pounding and his teeth feeling oddly loose. He shook his head, clearing the cobwebs, and forced his eyes open. He was still in the room, with nothing apparently changed. He located Grond, a few feet away, also sprawled on the floor.

Wait. One thing had changed. The halfogre was stark naked.

Brazel looked down. He was naked too. He sat up, pulling himself into a crouch, scanning the room. Other than the two of them, it was empty.

The ship. His comm link with the *Nameless* was mostly subcutaneous, hooked into the bones of his ears. It was still there. He tried to reach the ship. Nothing.

Grond staggered to his feet, growling, a deep bass rumble that Brazel could feel in his chest. The halfogre's eyes glowed a dim red even in the bright light of the room.

"The fuck happened?" he grumbled.

"I think she disintegrated our stuff or something," Brazel said. He fluffed his fur, looking and smelling for singed parts. Everything looked and smelled fine. *How the hell did she pull that off?*

With a noxious slurping noise, the black material pulled back away from the doorway. The door clicked and slid partially open.

"Me first," the halfogre said, flexing his muscles and clenching his fists. "First thing I see, I'm gonna beat it to death. Just so's you know." The gnome nodded.

They had entered the structure from the hollow interior of an enormous spacecraft. The doorway opened into what looked for all the world like a lobby in a pricey resort. There was expensive-looking furniture scattered about the room, artworks from various cultures adorning the walls, thick plush carpeting at their feet. The ceiling, six or seven meters high at least, was painted a deep blue, scattered with hundreds of twinkling lights, imitating a starlit sky. In the middle of the room was an enormous, free-standing firepit, where some sort of scented wood blazed away merrily; a grand staircase in the back of the room led to both higher and lower floors. A few feet in front of them sat an ornate square table made of some sort of elaborately carved hardwood, two paper-wrapped packages sitting atop it. The packages were wrapped with festive ribbons.

"You might beat the hell out of an end table, I suppose," Brazel volunteered. There was no one but the two of them in the room.

"This ain't right," Grond said. "Hologram? Hard-light? What do you think?"

"No idea." Brazel picked up the packages. His name was on the smaller one. He shook it; whatever was inside slid around like it was made of cloth. He locked eyes with Grond for a moment, who shrugged. Brazel tossed Grond the other package and opened his.

There was a robe inside, made of the softest cloth Brazel had ever laid hands on-- and the gnome had always had very expensive tastes in fabric. He put it on; it was sized perfectly. He tucked the ribbon into a pocket and glanced at Grond; the halfogre's package had included a robe as well.

"Now what?" he asked.

As if in answer, a panel slid aside in the ceiling and a 'bot flew into the room. It was a simple model, an oblong-shaped levitator with a couple of manipulator arms and a battery of sensors. The 'bot flew toward the pair, pausing a few meters in front of Grond, hovering at his eye level.

"Greetings," it intoned, in a softly feminine human voice. "You are--"

Grond hurled the table their robes had been on directly at the 'bot. The heavy table knocked the thing out of the air and then landed on it, crushing it to scrap metal. The 'bot squawked once in alarm and then quieted.

"Did that make you feel better?" Brazel asked.

"The next one had better have Angela with it," the halfogre muttered, his eyes still glowing dangerously.

The next one did not have Angela with it. It did have two impressive-looking projectile cannons on it, however, one trained on Brazel and the other on Grond.

"Greetings," it spoke, in the same voice. "You are in no danger. Please follow me."

"Those guns don't say *in no danger* to me," Brazel muttered. The 'bot made no response, but hovered backward toward the staircase, keeping its guns aimed carefully the entire time. The 'bot led them up the staircase, down a corridor in a far corner of the room and eventually down another stairwell, ignoring a number of other rooms and side paths along the way. *This place is huge*, Brazel thought. *What the hell's going on? How long were we unconscious?* It finally stopped outside a set of double doors, which swung open.

"The mistress will be with you shortly," the 'bot said. "Please wait inside."

Brazel glanced over at Grond. The halfogre had lost all of the red in his eyes, which were wide and staring. They were being led into a *library*. And, judging from the smell, most of the books were printed on actual paper, and not the thin polymer sheets that most of the physical books still available were created from. The shelves were stuffed full, running from the floor to the ceiling, with a half-dozen or so freestanding shelves scattered around the room as well. There were *thousands* of books.

"Uh ... Grond?" Brazel said. "Stay with me, buddy. We still don't actually know what's going on here, right?"

"Don't care anymore," Grond said. He picked a book off the shelf and leafed through it, leaning in and inhaling the scent of the pages. "She can kill us both so long as she gives me a couple of hours in here first. She can kill *you* whenever, actually." The halfogre looked around, spotting a lounge chair his size on the other side of the room, near yet another fireplace. There was a second chair next to it, this one not sized for bigs.

How much time did Remember have to customize her furniture for us? Brazel thought. If they were actually in Remember's home, it would make sense for most of her furniture to be sized for humans, or ... well, human-*sized* people, at least, which Remember supposedly was. Grond's chair barely creaked as he settled his nearly two-and-a-half meter frame into it; the thing *had* to be reinforced. It wasn't human furniture.

Seeing no better alternative, Brazel sat down in his chair and watched the fire.

"We have a game plan here?" he asked.

"We don't," Grond said. "I assume you've tried to contact the ship already. Either our comms are blocked or the ship is destroyed, near as I can tell. We're unarmed. I wrecked one of her robots and she sent a bigger one with *guns*. I don't see that we've got much of a choice but to sit here and see what she wants. Meanwhile..."

He waved the book, which looked positively dainty in his hands. "May as well relax until we find out why we're here."

"You're here because I have a task for you to perform," the fire said.

Grond and Brazel both sat up straight in their seats.

The fire shaped itself into a person.

That's impressive, Brazel thought.

As he watched, the fire-person's appearance refined, becoming something more like a holographic projection than a manipulation of the flame. It was a woman; a bit less than two meters tall, slightly above average for a human female, with long hair twisted into a topknot and then flowing down her back to below her waist. She appeared to be dressed in a loose, flowing robe, much like what had been provided for the two of them. Her hands were clasped behind his back.

Brazel and Grond waited. The fire-woman made no movement.

"Courtesy dictates that you explain the task. And perhaps introduce yourself," Brazel said.

"I am Remember," the fire-woman said. Her voice was surprisingly low, raspy. "My apologies for not meeting with you more ... personally."

"And the part where you destroyed all our stuff," said Grond, his eyes glittering red again. He had the book in his lap, holding it in such a way as to make Brazel think he planned to throw it. The gnome noticed the ribbon from their robe package marking a page. *He's not throwing that book,* Brazel thought. The chair would go first. Neither seemed terribly useful against a hologram made of *fire*, though.

"Your things are where you left them," Remember said.

"You knocked us out dressed and armed and we woke up naked," Brazel said. "I didn't *leave* my clothes anywhere. I rarely meet with business contacts naked. Tends to make me a trifle more difficult to take seriously."

"As I said, where you left them," Remember said. "*You* are not where you were when you were dressed and armed." She gestured and the room darkened, a star chart popping into existence in the middle of the library. Two stars glowed green.

"That's Queris," Brazel said, looking at one of the green dots. "And the other?"

"Is you," Remember said.

Brazel and Grond both laughed. The two points were halfway across the galaxy from each other; they had to be fifteen or twenty *parsecs* apart.

"That's a month. In tunnelspace," Brazel said. "You didn't have us unconscious for a month."

"You were unconscious for twelve seconds," Remember said.

Grond actually dropped his book.

"That's impossible," the halfogre said. "Teleportation?"

"It requires a ... moderate expenditure of power," Remember said. "I chose not to bring your possessions along with you. One of you might have chosen to bring something ... *unwise*." She stared at Brazel as she said that last word, making it clear that she knew exactly how many *unwise somethings* Brazel had tried to bring with him. Grond carried all of his tools openly; the halfogre felt that concealing weaponry was pointless. An easy belief, when you were as large as he was.

"Okay, so, we're impressed," Brazel said. *And you're lying*, he thought. There was no way Remember had *teleported* them. "You have access to a technology that as far as we know exists nowhere else in the galaxy and you've used it to move the two of us halfway across that galaxy so that you could *mysterious* at us out of a fireplace. Let's talk about the *job*, Remember."

Brazel wasn't sure, but he thought the fire-face grinned. "A relatively simple task, actually; I will be monitoring to see how well you follow your instructions, and there will be more complicated jobs for you in the future if you perform well. There is a certain package; I wish it to be delivered to a certain place. Twenty-five days later, I wish for you to retrieve it."

"We're not messing with Benevolence," Brazel said.

"The location I wish the package delivered to is not within Benevolence space," Remember responded.

"How much?" Grond asked.

Remember named a figure. An *enormous* figure.

"We're in," Brazel said. He signaled to Grond, a brief gesture that meant *not now— we'll discuss this later*.

"I am glad to hear it," Remember said. "Grond may keep the books, as well, if he wishes."

The halfogre's eyes cleared immediately. "B.... *books*? Plural?"

Remember's hologram smiled again, and bowed. The shape dissolved back into the fire.

Grond found a few boxes neatly stacked outside the library and insisted on spending an hour carefully going through everything in Remember's library, an hour during which he was lost in literary bliss and the gnome did his best to avoid going out of his mind from impatience. He refused to help transport the boxes back to the teleporter; Grond laughed at the notion.

"They're heavier than you," he said. "I think I can handle it."

The 'bot waiting for them when they finally left the library was an identical copy of the one Grond had crushed; Brazel noticed it seemed to be trying to keep its distance. It led them back to the lobby and the door to the teleporter slid open. There was a small table just inside with two glasses of blue liquid on it.

"Drink," it said. "And when you get inside, lie down. The fluid and lying prone will help with the teleportation. You will find all of your effects waiting for you when you arrive. We will send the books in ten minutes, along with the lady Remember's package. The package will give you the coordinates for the delivery. And you will find, by the way, that your ship has been refueled."

Grond shrugged and downed his drink. Brazel inspected his before drinking; other than the oddly bright color there was nothing unusual looking about it. It tasted like a combination of especially strong tea and finely ground, blueberry-flavored gravel.

I've paid for worse, he thought as he finished. He'd learned, over the years, to never let his partner pick the drinks.

Teleporting while conscious was somewhat more pleasant than the alternative; the black material holding him still for only a few seconds, the teleportation itself loud but otherwise painless. Brazel had thought he'd be able to pinpoint the exact moment at which they jumped, but if he really was jumping parsecs across the galaxy he certainly couldn't feel it happening.

True to the 'bot's word, their gear, Angela included, was waiting for them and the boxes of books came through precisely ten minutes after they arrived. Remember's package was a metallic case, perhaps a meter square by just under two meters long. There was a blank screen in the middle of the top of the case and a single button; handles were built into the side. Grond stacked his books on top of the case and crouched to pick it up.

And grunted, exhaling explosively. The box didn't move.

"No way," the halfogre muttered, and moved the books, trying the case by itself. He couldn't budge it. He moved to one end, gripping the handle and trying to lift from the end. Brazel watched, half-amused, as veins stood out on the halfogre's neck and arms and his legs strained to try and budge the box.

"You're gonna pull something," the gnome said. "Or ... well, not, maybe."

"You fucking pick it up then," Grond said, letting go of the handle and straightening up. Brazel looked over the case carefully, then pushed the button. The screen lit up with what were clearly coordinates-- one set indicating their current location in the Queris system, and a second that Brazel didn't immediately recognize. A soft buzz came from inside and it lifted a few feet off the ground. Brazel poked it with a finger and it slid toward the door. He waved a hand underneath the box. There was nothing happening underneath to indicate how it was being lifted.

He risked making eye contact with his partner, who snorted and made a rude gesture.

"Teleportation and portable antigrav," he said. "What the hell's she need us for?" Antigravity rigs weren't uncommon, necessarily; lots of ships used them and certain larger 'bots, but they were generally expensive and much, *much* bulkier than whatever was inside this box had to be.

With a brief burst of static, his comm reestablished contact with the *Nameless*.

YOU'RE BACK, the ship said.

"We are," Brazel said. "How long were we gone?" He pushed the antigrav rig out of the teleportation room, Grond following him with the books.

I LOST COMMUNICATION WITH YOU ONE HOUR AND FORTY-SEVEN MINUTES AGO, the ship responded. FIFTEEN MINUTES AGO THE SPHERE BEGAN POWERING BACK UP AGAIN. I SURMISED THAT WHATEVER PROCESS HAD CAUSED US TO LOSE CONTACT WAS ABOUT TO BE REVERSED.

"Teleporter," Brazel said. "We were on the other side of the galaxy."

IMPRESSIVE, Namey responded. THE AMOUNT OF POWER GENERATED BY THE SPHERE IS LIKELY SUFFICIENT TO HAVE TRANSPORTED THE TWO OF YOU, PROVIDED THAT THE TECHNOLOGY TO DO SO WAS AVAILABLE. I WAS NOT AWARE THAT THAT WAS THE CASE.

"Apparently so," Brazel said. "Get the cargo hold open; we'll be there in a minute."

⊰⊙⊱

As soon as they had their new cargo safely stowed, Brazel and Grond checked the coordinates that they were to deliver the package to. They identified a planet in a relatively unpopulated area of gnomespace, not far from home and more or less along their way.

"See what you can find out about that planet," Brazel told Namey. "And turn the dampers on in this room for the next ten minutes." The AI signed off noiselessly, and Brazel waited a moment for the communication dampers in the room to kick in.

"So. What's her game?"

"The books are bugged, aren't they?" Grond asked.

"Probably," Brazel responded. "Although it's not like she doesn't know where we're going, and it's not like the package itself isn't a giant homing beacon screaming HERE WE ARE halfway across the galaxy. But, yeah, I'd bet there's nanotrackers in a bunch of those books. Where'd you put them?"

"In the cargo hold," Grond said. "I'll have Namey scan the hell out of them before they go anywhere else in the ship, though. Maybe I accidentally throw them into an EMP field at some point. By *accident*. And maybe once we land they don't go anywhere else after that."

"Probably best," Brazel said. "What do you think's in the box?"

"I've been thinking about that," Grond said. "No idea. I halfway wonder if there's actually anything in there in the first place. This whole thing scans like some sort of elaborate test, and I can't figure her angle. We're small-time; there's no reason for Remember to have noticed us unless we screwed her first. And bringing us to her to talk for ten minutes then send us back and put us on an overpaid courier job makes me think maybe she needs an accountant. We could buy a whole new ship to move that box in for what she's paying us. It's insane."

"We're not *that* small-time," Brazel complained. Grond shrugged.

"We can have Namey scan the box, too," Brazel added, "Remember didn't say anything about not opening it or anything like that; she just said *take it here* and then *go back and get it*. She didn't seem too concerned about what we did with it in the meantime."

"He won't find anything," Grond said. "We know this, right?"

"We do," Brazel agreed. "I don't like this job, though. I don't like it at all. We're being paid too much to do too simple of a job, and both of those things scream it's a trap to me. And it's not even a good trap; if she'd wanted us dead, I'm sure that 'bot wasn't the only dangerous thing she could have turned loose on us."

"Look on the bright side," Grond said. "Twenty-five days from now we're either dead, which means no more worrying about it, or we're very, very rich. I figure I can live with either of those."

"I don't need to tell you to keep your eyes peeled, I assume," Brazel said.

"I always do," the halfogre rumbled, chuckling. "Unlike you, I can see over the furniture, so I sort of have to be the one looking out for everything."

A series of scans and a thorough electromagnetic decontamination later, Grond's books were pronounced safe and they were no closer to determining the contents of Remember's case. Brazel and Grond mutually decided to not worry about it. They were three days away from the system, which was called Gallireen, after the largest planet of the system, a jumble of mid-sized terrestrials mostly too close to the star to be terribly hospitable for life and a handful of gas giants. The exact location was on a moon of one of the inner gas planets, which according to Namey's databases, housed a few hardscrabble settlements and some minor green areas but was mostly desert and stone, pulling enough heat and light to survive from the huge planet it orbited. Namey called it Gallireen 12A; the locals no doubt had some other name for it.

"Looks like ... huh," Brazel said, paging through the database. Grond raised an eyebrow.

"Mostly *human* settlements," he continued. "Even though the planet's in gnomespace. Not a lot of native humans in gnomespace. That tell you anything?"

"Smugglers," Grond responded. "Or outcasts. Or both. Outcasts who became smugglers. Also means I might actually be able to sit at the bar, if we find one."

"Don't get your hopes up," Brazel responded. "I doubt we'll be there long enough for a drink. I want this job over and done with as quick as we can; if we're on this rock for more than an hour it'll mean something's gone wrong."

Grond just grinned.

"Okay, fine, and I refuse to use a booster seat in my own damn neck of the galaxy;" Brazel snapped. "Plus, hell, I'd like to get home sooner or later. That way you can be the wrong size for all the furniture for once."

He cued up the coordinates and the *Nameless* fell into tunnelspace.

The trip passed uneventfully; Grond had already worked his way through three of his new books by the time the *Nameless* emerged from tunnelspace a few hundred thousand kilometers from their destination.

INSTRUCTIONS FOR APPROACH? Namey asked.

"Any reason we need to be particularly careful with this one?"

NONE, the AI responded.   NO NOTICEABLE MILITARY PRESENCE AND NO BENEVOLENCE SIGNALS OR STANDARD CODE FREQUENCIES IN USE.

"One of the more common identities, then," Brazel responded. "Just pick one."

There was a moment of silence as the *Nameless* negotiated with Gallireen 12A for permission to dock.

GRANTED.   THERE   IS   COMMERCIAL DOCKING SPACE AVAILABLE WITHIN EASY REACH OF OUR DESTINATION.

Brazel breathed a sigh of relief.   He'd been concerned about that; his maps of Gallireen 12A were not especially detailed and he'd been concerned that the nearest docking facilities that could handle the *Nameless* were going to be on the wrong side of the planet from wherever they were supposed to drop off Remember's package— which meant two round-trips on planet, since they'd have to recover the box as well. The *Nameless* could land on rough terrain in a pinch, but if anything the gnome was pickier about his ship than he was his clothes; he didn't like risking the ship to substandard landing conditions unless the job absolutely demanded it.

"Bring us in," he said. "Who are we, by the way?"

THE *HAMSTRINGER*, OUT OF THE OKRASTER SYSTEM, the ship responded.   ON PLANET ON BUSINESS. LENGTH OF STAY, TWO STANDARD WEEKS. NO ONE ASKED YOUR NAMES; CALL YOURSELVES WHATEVER YOU WANT.

"Works for me. Where's the box going?"

THE BASEMENT OF A COMMERCIAL
BUILDING WITHIN EASY WALKING DISTANCE
OF THE SPACEPORT.

"We're couriers, then," Brazel said. "You get the
feeling anyone's paying attention to the spaceport?"

THEY ARE BEING EXCEPTIONALLY SUBTLE
ABOUT IT IF THEY ARE, the ship responded. THE
PORT AI WAS BORED. I DIDN'T THINK
ARTIFICIAL INTELLIGENCES GOT BORED.

"I didn't think they used contractions."

EVERY SO OFTEN I LIKE TO SHAKE THINGS
UP.

"Wake up the halfogre, then. He's got recon to do."

Brazel had never understood how it was possible
that his partner— his former gladiator, heavily tattooed,
scarred, two-point-four-meters-tall halfogre *partner*—
was so much better at going unnoticed than he was.
Grond had walked through rooms full of gnomish
children more than once without any of them noticing
he was even there. He had the uncanny ability to blend
in *anywhere*, right up to the point where he *wanted* to
attract attention— and few were better than he was at
that, either. Grond walked off the ship dressed in well-
worn laborer's clothes, Angela folded up and concealed
under a jacket and no more than seven or eight knives
concealed on his person.

He was back within an hour.

"This really is the easiest job ever," he said.
"There's a back door into the building straight into a
stairwell, and get this— only the two top floors of the

building are even *occupied*; some kind of medical research company— and there aren't even any windows facing the back. There's an alley in between it and another building and neither of them have any windows facing each other. And the two of them are the two tallest structures in the neighborhood. I coulda had the case dropped off already if I'd thought to bring it with me. I like this place; everybody minds their own business."

"I'm still going with you for the drop," the gnome said.

"May as well," Grond said. "You hang back, though; I'm gonna look like I'm carrying the box. Nobody anywhere is gonna believe that a halfogre needs help from a gnome to move something heavy."

Brazel nodded. "I'll watch your back," he said.

Grond had been right— the trip to the drop spot took no more than a fifteen-minute walk and neither Grond nor Brazel attracted anything more than a stray glance or two along the way. The alley between the buildings was slightly narrower and *much* higher than Brazel liked— they were trapped if for some reason they had to fight their way out of the building— but Grond cracked the lock in moments and they were inside the building quickly. The back door opened into a stairwell.

"Downstairs," Brazel said. "Coordinates are a bit underground."

"You think we're supposed to hide the thing, or…?" Grond asked.

"We're supposed to leave it here for 25 days," Brazel responded. "Stands to reason we probably ought to make sure nobody moves it before then. Let's see if there's a storeroom or something down there."

A few minutes of searching produced a likely spot; the lower levels of the building were clearly disused and the pair quickly found a lockable closet in a part of the floor that felt out of the way.

"That work for you?"

"Yeah," Brazel said. "Let's get out of here."

Neither of them heard the device begin to hum as they closed the door behind them.

Being paid to laze about on Arradon, Brazel found, was very much to his liking. With nothing in particular to do during Remember's specified 25 days, and unlimited access to the resort his wife owned a partial stake in, he found himself taking a lot of long baths and spending a lot of time relaxing and playing with his children.

The peace and quiet lasted precisely ten days.

"We have a problem," Rhundi said.

"I don't have a problem yet," Brazel responded. He was neck-deep in a hot scented bath and very much not in a temper where "problems" were possible things for him. *"I* only have a problem if you give me one." *Please do not give me a problem*, he thought.

"What was the name of the planet you dropped Remember's box off at?" she asked.

Brazel thought about it. "One of the Gallireens, I think. 11A? 12B? I don't remember. Ask the boat."

"12A, right?"

"Sure," he replied. *This can't be good.*

"It isn't," she said, reading his mind. Rhundi and Brazel had been married for *quite* a long time and had had conversations very much like this many times.

"And it's not a problem I can fix from the bath, is it?" he asked, sighing. It never was.

"Plague," she said.

He got out of the bath.

"First cases were reported seven days ago," she said. Brazel had made himself dry, dressed and presentable in record time, and Rhundi was reading reports from her desk console in her office. "And as of right now it's spread over a third of the moon. They've estimated something like four thousand cases on a rock that only has a population of about twenty times that many people. Most of them are in the neighborhood of a city called Rua'ta."

She paused for a moment. "Two guesses where you dropped off the package."

"I never even found out the name of the town," Brazel said. "We were just following the coordinates. Fuck, I knew there was gonna be a catch."

"It gets worse," she said. "The plague is a technovirus. It's internally networked. The victims are flocking, like birds, and they're actively seeking out new victims to infect. That's how it moves so fast. If the Benevolence finds out there's going to be an interdiction."

"They'll wipe out the entire fucking moon," Brazel said.

"Likely," she responded. "The virus doesn't seem to be smart enough right now to animate its victims to do much more than seek out other people to infect. But we don't know what will happen if it continues to infect more people. If the thing ends up being a distributed AI, and if it gets smarter as it gets more widespread..."

"It eventually figures out how to make someone pilot a boat, it packs as many infected as it can into the holds, and it heads somewhere with a lot more people," Brazel said.

"Thus the interdiction," Rhundi said. "Death sentence for the entire planet. And everything on it. I told you this job was a bad idea."

"You did not," Brazel responded. "I specifically remember never asking you."

"You knew I thought it," she snapped. "Remember's bad news, and we never should have gotten into business with her."

"Do we know it's the box?"

"The first cases were *three days* after you dropped off the box, in the *same city* you dropped the box off in," Rhundi responded. "You do the math."

"Never liked math much," Brazel said. "Ask Grond."

"Grond agrees," the halfogre said, lowering his head to get through the door. There was a single chair in Rhundi's office sized for him, and he collapsed into it. "You don't like math much, *and* this is our fault. We never shoulda taken this job, Braze."

"Right, because you were totally arguing against it," the gnome said, disgusted. "How is this suddenly my fault?"

"It's not," Rhundi said, laying her hand on her husband's arm and smoothing his fur. "But we're going to do something about it."

"What?" Brazel asked. "Seriously, what can we do about it?   Slip back onto the planet before the Benevolence find out and blow it to pieces and then deactivate the box or something?"

Grond grinned.

"*Stop grinning*. That is not a plan," Brazel said. "That is fucking madness and you know it. How the hell do we even get close to the thing without getting infected ourselves?"

"That we should be able to handle," Rhundi said. "I can get ahold of some gear. Just... try not to bleed. Or breathe too much."

Brazel glared at his wife.

"Eighty thousand people, Brazel," Rhundi said. "I can't have that on my conscience. Neither can Grond. And even if you won't admit it, neither can you."

"We could just tell the Benevolence where the case is," he said.

"Which would let them know where *we* are," she retorted, "and wouldn't you *love* to explain to the Benevolence how you *know* where the source of a technovirus is? Or that you knew there was a source in the first place? You're delicate, Brazel. You wouldn't last half a day under Benevolence interrogation."

"Okay, that was stupid," Brazel said. "I admit it. But ... really. You want us to, what, blow the box apart? Will that kill the virus? Or just stop it from replicating?"

"I don't know," Rhundi said. "Yet. But I've got my people working on it already. We'll have something for you in a day or so. Right now, start prepping the *Nameless*. You two have work to do."

Brazel and Grond both stood up.

"Oh, and Brazel?"

"Yeah?"

"Shuni's birthday is next week. You may want to spend some time with her before you leave."

"I *knew* that," Brazel said. "I've even got a gift picked out."

"Good. Also, Grond?"

"I know," the halfogre rumbled. "Bring him back alive."

Rhundi nodded, a smile barely touching her eyes, and went back to work at her console.

"*I feel compelled to point out* that we *still* do not have a plan," Brazel said a day later as the *Nameless* dropped into tunnelspace.

"We're making some assumptions," Grond said agreeably.

"We're making nothing *but* assumptions," Brazel responded. "We're assuming that we had anything to do with this. We're assuming that destroying the box or getting it off-planet will do anything other than *spread the virus further* if we're right about it being our fault. We're assuming that we can do this before the Benevolence show up and ruin our day and everyone else's. And we're assuming that we can slip into a technovirus-infected planet that is presumably full of violent nanobot-driven innocent people and do *all of this* without getting infected *ourselves*."

"Sounds like a tall order, when ya put it that way," Grond said.

"Don't you get all folksy with me," Brazel snapped.

The comm chirped. It was Rhundi.

"Good news," she said. "Well, mostly good news. My engineers think they can find a way to turn the virus off. All you have to do is get them a sample of it." Brazel spent a moment reflecting on the phrase *my engineers*. His wife's business dealings had always been well beyond him; she had been every bit the smuggler he was when they'd met but was almost entirely legitimate now. He'd not realized that she'd gotten into anything that involved employing *engineers*.

"You say that as if *get them a sample of it* and *all you have to do* belong in the same sentence. Tell me *exactly* what that means," Brazel said.

"Grab one of the infected people, get a blood sample, drop it into the nanoanalytics unit I had installed on the *Nameless* before you left, comm us the results," she said. "Try not to kill the infected person while you're getting blood from them. Also, try not to let them bleed on you. Or on the ship. There's not enough news coming off the planet to let us be sure exactly how the virus transmits itself. Also, don't breathe unless you're wearing a respirator. Those are on the ship too. Hopefully my gals get back to you with a kill signal before your position becomes inconvenient."

"Easy," Grond rumbled.

"And blow the box along the way," she said. "We're figuring that if Grond couldn't lift the thing without the antigrav pads on, it's not too likely that he's going to be able to move it now unless it wants to be moved. My people figure it's manufacturing the virus and pumping it into the air. If we cut off the source and then shut down everything that's in the wild, we'll have saved the planet."

"Another understatement," Brazel said. "Any word on Benevolence?"

"No movement yet," she said. "The planet's out of the way and a lot closer to us than it is to them. You won't have a ton of time once they find out and take action, though; the first thing they'll do is drop a blockship into the neighborhood to keep travelers from entering tunnelspace and the next step is to blow up anything that tries to leave the planet or get too close to it.   It won't be pretty.   Then... boom.   We're monitoring, though."

"Okay," he said. "Anything else?"

"You've also got a few cases of stun ammo. Try to use that instead of anything lethal unless you don't have a choice. And seriously, don't die," she said. "I'm too busy for dating right now and replacing you would be a pain."

"You remain the light of my existence, dear," Brazel said and signed off.

They spent most of the trip modifying their weaponry to use Rhundi's stun ammunition. This was a simple process for a single gun, but Grond tended to carry a lot of guns on the ship and insisted on modifying virtually everything before they arrived. "Never know what tool you'll need," he said when Brazel called him out on it. "Don't really wanna kill someone on account of being too lazy to reset my guns on the way."

"What if you *do* need to kill someone?"

Grond pointed at a wall full of bladed weapons. "I do it up close," he said. "And I can switch Angela over in a coupla seconds; those Iklis weapons are built to be versatile. We'll be fine."

"If you say so," Brazel said.

APPROACHING THE GALLIREEN SYSTEM, Namey announced. DOCKING FACILITIES PLANETWIDE ON GALLIREEN 12A ARE BROADCASTING LOOPED EMERGENCY MESSAGES. WE ARE INSTRUCTED THAT WE ARE NOT TO LAND UNDER ANY CIRCUMSTANCES.

"Do it anyway," Brazel said. "Or at least get in close. Let's do a flyover of Rua'ta and see what it looks like down there."

Namey clicked an acknowledgement and the *Nameless* closed in on the moon.

"She was right, it's like watching birds," Grond said. The *Nameless* was hovering a klick or so above Rua'ta, and even from that distance, viewing a holoprojection, it was easy to tell that something was terribly wrong in the city. It had looked sparsely populated on their first visit; this time, nearly everyone

was *outside*. From above the patterns were clear; there were knots of people standing virtually still, while others roved in large groups of perhaps thirty or forty, moving together in what almost looked like purposeful formation. Every so often one of the still groups would all move at once, relocating— at what looked like top speed— to some other location, then freezing in place again.

"There's the office building." Grond tapped the image once and the building they'd left the box in lit up. "That's... uh, that's not good."

"How many do you think there are?" Brazel asked.

I ESTIMATE FOUR HUNDRED, Namey added helpfully.

The building was completely surrounded with people, who didn't appear to be doing anything other than endlessly circling it in a manner that reminded Brazel less of birds and more of insects in a death spiral. There was clearly no way to approach the place from the ground.

"Namey, any way to estimate the number of people who aren't infected down there?"

ONLY INDIRECTLY, the ship responded. THERE ARE THREE THOUSAND SEVEN HUNDRED AND THREE STANDARD-TYPE LIFE FORMS OUTDOORS WITHIN TWO KILOMETERS OF OUR COORDINATES RIGHT NOW. THE POPULATION OF RUA'TA WAS ROUGHLY SIX THOUSAND A MONTH AGO.

"So two thousand people uninfected, *maybe*, assuming all the plague victims are in the flocks outdoors," Brazel murmured. "That's ... an awful lot of people."

THIS ASSUMES NO CASUALTIES AS WELL. THE TECHNOVIRUS IS DESIGNED TO SPREAD ITSELF, NOT TO KILL, BUT SURELY THE UNINFECTED WOULD HAVE FOUGHT BACK. THE ROVING GROUPS APPEAR TO BE PATROLLING; THEY MAY HAVE CLEARED UNINFECTED FROM THE AREA AROUND THE BOX ALREADY.   THERE ARE SCATTERED POCKETS OF LIFE FORMS INSIDE SOME STRUCTURES AROUND RUA'TA BUT I HAVE NO WAY TO DETERMINE THEIR STATUS AS INFECTED OR UNINFECTED.

"Still a lot of people," Brazel said. "Now would be the time to hear about your plan, Grond."

"Drop me on a roof nearby," Grond said. "Then come get me when I need you to."

"You're *kidding*," Brazel said.

"Not a bit," Grond said. "Somebody's gotta fly the ship; you're a better pilot than I am. And it's nuts to try to get there on the ground. That leaves the windows or the roof."

"And *when* they see us and come into the building to find you?"

"So distract them," Grond said. "Namey's got external loudspeakers.   Make the loudest most obnoxious sound you can and then fly a few blocks away. See if you can get them to follow you. If not, I'll manage."

"Or we could just *bomb the building*. That seems a trifle safer."

"For us. There's a few hundred people that are gonna get *landed on* if you do that. And the box is in the basement. No guarantee that dropping the rest of the place on top of it is even going to do any good. We're not Benevolence. We're not killing four hundred people today even if we think it saves more than that."

"Tell me you're at least suiting up."

"Completely," Grond said, holding up an envirosuit. "Rhundi had this thing custom-made. There's even *holsters* built into it. She's thoughtful, that wife of yours. You oughtta treat her nicer."

"*You* treat her nicer," Brazel grumbled. The halfogre was right, though. He had a much better chance of getting in and out than Brazel did, and both of them leaving the ship was crazy.

COMPLICATION, Namey said.

"Of course there is," Brazel answered.

THERE ARE ALREADY LIFE FORMS IN THE TARGET BUILDING, the ship responded. ALL ON THE TOP FLOORS. MOST BUILDINGS IN THE AREA ARE ABANDONED.

"I thought you said they'd cleared everything?"

CONJECTURE. THEY MAY HAVE MISSED SURVIVORS IN THE BUILDING OR THESE MAY BE INFECTED.

"Are there less than four hundred of them?" Grond said.

THERE ARE LESS THAN A DOZEN.

"I'll survive," the halfogre said, pulling on his envirosuit. "Braze, get me near that building across the alley. Do a nice slow pass and I'll jump out; if we get lucky they won't even realize that anyone left the boat. Then make a bunch of noise and fly off somewhere else. Maybe they'll follow you, maybe they won't; either way if they're not looking at the roof I ought to be able to get across and into the building. Wait for me to comm you back and come get me. Easy."

"Famous last words," the gnome said.

"Nah. My last words are probably gonna be *much* more profane than that. I've always figured 'Oh, *fuck!*' would be the last thing I ever said," Grond responded.

"Quit telling jokes and head for the cargo hold," Brazel said. "I hope your timing's good. You're not going to enjoy the fall if you miss your jump."

Grond slung his longbow over his back and grinned.

"I won't miss if you can fly straight," he said.

Grond didn't miss, and the halfogre fell into a forward roll as soon as he hit the rooftop, stopping his momentum before running into anything solid. He rolled to his feet, a heavy projectile pistol loaded with stun darts in one hand and a heavy knife in the other. He looked around. There was nothing alive anywhere near him. He flinched as the wall of sound from the *Nameless* hit him; Brazel seemed to be playing every audio file on the boat at once at the highest volume Namey's external speakers could handle. Hopefully it would draw some attention.

He took a moment to be briefly grateful that the two buildings were the same height. The gap between them was about eight feet wide; in the alley below, the mass of plague victims was already starting to separate and clear. None of them appeared to be looking up. He took a running start and cleared it easily.

Need a way in. There was an access door in the northwest corner of the building, right over the door they'd used to get in from the alley. The stairwell, presumably, would go all the way down to the basement. Convenient. He spent a moment thinking about the best way to get the door open quietly and then laughed at himself; the *Nameless* was still making so much noise that nothing short of explosives would made a difference.

Also, it was unlocked, as he discovered when he tested the handle. He opened the door slowly anyway, widening the gap just far enough to squeeze his huge frame inside the doorway. *Good thing the planet's sized for bigs,* he thought. It was too dark to see inside; he felt his way down the stairs to the top floor and then waited, listening carefully. Namey had said there were less than a dozen people inside. That meant he'd assume twenty.

He couldn't hear a thing.

It was too easy the first time, he thought. Maybe he'd get lucky again. He gave his eyes another minute or two to adjust to the darkness, adjusted his respirator over his mouth and nose, then started making his way downstairs.

He made it almost an entire floor before all hell broke loose.

Something exploded on the floor beneath him, blowing the door on the landing beneath him off its hinges and into the stairwell. A small form stumbled through the doorway, coughing and wiping its eyes— a human female, it looked like— and then shook her head as if to clear the cobwebs and fled down the stairs. A moment later a scrum of other humans flowed through the doorway and down the stairs after her. "Flowed" was the only word for it— at the speed they were moving, they should have been running into and stumbling over each other, but not one of them made contact with anyone else as they came out and headed down. There were glowing blue lines tracing over their exposed hands and faces; their features were distressingly calm. Not one of them made a sound. And not one of them noticed Grond as he shrank back into the upper floor.

Shit. He had enough to do without adding a rescue. At least they were headed the right way. He heard a scream from below, thumbed Angela into stun mode and hurled himself through the smoke and down the stairs.

The woman was fighting for her life against a crowd of infected, a short stun baton in one hand and a crackling electroblade in the other. Grond dropped two of them with two shots in the back before they noticed he was there, their bodies slumping harmlessly to the floor. One turned its head to look his way and then, moving as one, the *entire group* disengaged itself from the first fight to focus on him.

"You've gotta be fucking kidding me," he said, retreating and shooting two more. The woman, meanwhile, turned and fled back down the stairs without a word to Grond.

"HEY!" he shouted, assessing his situation. They'd be on him in a moment; he wouldn't be able to shoot fast enough.

Nonlethal methods be damned; it was time for blades. He threw Angela onto his back and drew two of them; either would be a sword in Brazel's hands but looked like long daggers in his. He didn't have the room for anything bigger. The victims were unarmed, but there were a lot of them and he needed to keep his envirosuit undamaged. The woman hadn't been wearing one; he wondered if she was infected yet or not.

Circumstances aside, though, one armed and skilled halfogre against what turned out to be nine unarmed humans did not end up being a long fight. Their motions were coordinated but it was clear that none were warriors and Grond was able to put all of them down in a couple of minutes of intense fighting. *Pretty sure a few of them aren't even dead,* he thought. A few would need to learn occupations that didn't involve having two arms, though.

Back down the stairs. This time he made it three floors down before the woman barreled into him, coming *back up again* and around the corner. She swung the stun baton at him and he grabbed her wrist, the baton flying out of her hand and bouncing harmlessly off the wall.

"Who the hell *are* you?" he asked.

"No time," she said. "They're coming."

Pain exploded in Grond's right forearm, and he looked down to see a ten-inch gash torn through his suit and his arm as well. There were more of them coming— *lots* of them— and one had just thrown something sharp at him.

Shit. Networked. The ones outside found out about the fight inside. No amount of noise Brazel was going to make would distract them now. The woman wriggled out of his grasp and headed up the stairs. Grond grabbed the first infected to get close to him and hurled it at the rest of them, knocking a dozen or so people back down the stairs in a writhing, silent mass.

There was no way he was getting into the basement without killing his way through all of them, and he wasn't equipped for it. And his suit was compromised. The wound on his arm looked bad.

GROND, Brazel commed into his ear. UPSTAIRS. NOW. WE'RE ABORTING.

What?

"I was about to tell *you* that," Grond muttered, turning and fleeing. "What's *your* reason?"

THERE'S BENEVOLENCE ON THE OUTSKIRTS OF THE SYSTEM, Brazel responded. NAMEY SAYS WE'VE GOT FIVE MINUTES TO GET CLEAR BEFORE THE BLOCKSHIP GETS CLOSE ENOUGH TO KEEP US HERE.

The halfogre didn't need to hear anything else, making his way back to the roof in a matter of moments and locking the door behind him. The woman was still up there, eyeing the gap between the two buildings as if trying to decide if she was going to be able to jump it.

"Need a ride?" Grond asked. "One chance. Benevolence is coming; we're all dead in a few minutes."

"I've got a ride," she said.

"Unless it's fucking *invisible*, no, you don't," Grond said. He heard the wail of the *Nameless'* engines as Brazel brought the ship around, opening the cargo door and giving him room to jump in.

RIGHT NOW, GROND.

The two of them wasted no time with more words, turning and sprinting for the ship. Grond leapt, landing and rolling to safety in the cargo bay first. He heard and felt the woman land next to him. The cargo bay door groaned closed as Brazel streaked out of the moon's atmosphere.

"Stay here," he told the woman, locking the cargo hold behind himself and heading for his copilot's chair in his quarters. He threw himself into his chair, activated the holographic screens, and commed Brazel.

"You noticed we picked up a stray," he said.

"Tell me later," Brazel responded. "She look smart enough to figure out to hold on to something for the next couple of minutes?"

"She heard me say *Benevolence*," he responded. "I hope so."

"We're heading for the other side of the star," he said. "Namey doesn't think they've noticed us yet. Cross every finger you have that they don't or they'll probably come after us too."

His arm was still bleeding badly. *No time for that right now.* If the Benevolence sent spiderships after them they'd need him handling the guns, not in the closet that passed for the ship's medical bay. The long-range sensors showed two blockships and a sub-*Testament* class capital ship; they were definitely planning on an interdiction.

"How far?" he said.

"Just a couple minutes," Brazel responded. "We're not trying for tunnelspace if we can hide; they might notice the jump."

Grond waited. Watched the capital ship move into position near Gallireen 12A. Watched, as a sequence of energy blasts from the ship scorched the surface of the moon into flaming cinders, the sheer violence of the blasts tumbling it from orbit. The massive explosion when it inevitably fell into the planet would be visible from lightyears away.

They had failed.

They waited for hours on the other side of the sun, waiting for the Benevolence to leave the system, and then for a few more hours after that, just to make certain they were really gone. Grond sat, staring, the bleeding from the wound on his arm eventually slowing on its own, uncared for. Brazel wandered the ship, taking care of little maintenance jobs here and there that he'd not found time for but that suddenly seemed terribly important. They let the ship take care of their guest for a while, Brazel eventually bringing her some food himself just to have someone to talk to.

"She's asking for you, you know," Brazel said, braving his partner's quarters. Grond was sitting on his bunk, his arm still unbound, staring at a thin, lightweight shiv that he had balanced on one finger. It was the narrowest blade he owned, nearly useless for combat but perfectly balanced and easier than most to conceal. He could actually toss it from one finger to another without dropping it on a good day.

Grond said nothing.

"You're probably not infected," the gnome continued. "We'd know by now. Rhundi wants you to use the nanoanalyzer anyway. She's worried about you."

The halfogre spun the knife into his palm, reached into a drawer next to his bunk, and tossed something at Brazel. The gnome caught it, a surprised look on his face.

"It's ... a vial of blood. You have a vial of your own blood in a drawer next to your bed."

"I was gonna do it," Grond rumbled. "Just ... not ready to yet. Gimme a bit. Go run the blood; I'll be out in a few minutes. We'll talk to the girl and then decide what to do next."

"We did everything we could, Grond."

The halfogre stood up.

"Not yet," he said.

Her name was Ilana, and that was really all she had to say about anything. She was a female human, perhaps 25 years old, and amazingly slight for a human, perhaps only forty to fifty centimeters taller than Brazel. She'd willingly surrendered her electroblade and another smaller blade she'd had concealed in a boot; she said she had had a gun but had lost it in the battle before encountering Grond. She would say nothing on why she was on Gallireen, much less in the precise building that Grond and Brazel had left Remember's package in.

"So what do we do with you, then?" Grond asked, scratching at the bandage he'd finally put on his arm. "We could space you and be done with you. You're not telling us anything, which makes you hard to trust. I could *make* you tell us things. So could Brazel. But I feel like we've hurt enough people lately. So why don't you just tell us what you need."

"Just pick somewhere with a spaceport and drop me off," she said. "I'll figure it out from there. I can take care of myself."

"You'd be *dead* if I'd let you take care of yourself," Grond said. "And *I'd* be dead if I didn't have Brazel flying a ship for me. So can the solo act. But fine, you'll get what you want."

He turned to Brazel, who was standing just behind him. "We'll set up something comfortable in one of the bigger lockable cargo bays. She can stay there until we get somewhere civilized. You okay with that?"

The gnome nodded.

He turned to her. "You okay with that?"

She nodded.

"Fine, settled. Namey, where are we going?"

THERE ARE HALF A DOZEN ACCEPTABLE PLANETS WITHIN A DAY'S TUNNELSPACE FROM OUR CURRENT POSITION, the ship replied.

"Pick one on the way back home," Grond said. He looked at the other two. "We done here?"

No one spoke.

"Fine," he said. "I'll be in my bunk." He turned on one heel and left the room.

"Enjoy your stay on the *Nameless*, I suppose," Brazel said. "I'll be back in a bit. For right now, you're staying right here. The ship won't let you get anywhere outside the cargo hold. I'll bring you some bedding and a change of clothes once we're moving."

She remained silent.

"Have it your way," he said. "The halfogre's actually a pretty remarkable guy when he hasn't just had a planet blown up in front of him. I'm the one you need to worry about. He's upset that they're dead. I couldn't be happier that we're *alive*."

She smiled at that, just a bit.

"And you?"

"Both, I guess," she said. "Thank you for saving me. I owe you. But that doesn't mean we have to be friends."

"That's fair," Brazel said. "Mercenary, even. I like that in a person. I'll come back when I know where we're going."

He didn't even make it to the cockpit. Years of piloting the same boat had taught him to recognize the subtle shift in his body when the *Nameless* entered tunnelspace; most flyers couldn't tell you unless they happened to be watching or paying close attention when it happened.

Coming *out* of tunnelspace was something entirely different, especially when it happened at speed. Getting torn out of tunnelspace was *exquisitely* painful. It wasn't quite as unpleasant as the unexpected teleportation had been, but it was hard to imagine anything that was that didn't kill him or leave most of his insides somewhere new.

The ship stopped dead, too fast, faster than it ought to be able to. It overcame the inertial dampers and sent him flying into a wall.

"The fuck was that?"

There was no response from the *Nameless*.

Oh, fuck. "Namey. Say something. Grond, you out there?"

"Yeah," the halfogre said, sounding dazed. "I'm … holy shit, the AI's *rebooting* … Oh fuck. Get to the damn cockpit. The fucking teleporter. It's *outside.*"

"What the hell do you mean it's outside?"

"I mean Remember just yanked us out of tunnelspace, which means she's got her own blockship *built into* that thing, and she's not shooting at us yet but she *might start*," Grond yelled.

Brazel sprinted to the cockpit, ignoring pains from what seemed like half of his body. The grey facade of Remember's enormous teleporter filled the *Nameless'* viewscreen. The ship appeared to be listing to the side, drifting across the face of the sphere.

Wait. He checked their coordinates and gave the yoke an experimental twist. They weren't moving. The teleporter was *rotating*. The boat was still dead, immobile in space. He checked Namey's brainbox; Grond was right— he was rebooting. The last time the AI had had to reboot the boat had nearly been blown in *half*. And without the AI's help, he couldn't figure out why the ship couldn't move without manually checking the engines himself. He couldn't see any evidence of an inertia beam outside the ship, but that didn't necessarily mean anything.

The sphere rotated, and the docking port slowly came into view. With a jerk, the *Nameless* began moving again, pulled inexorably toward the landing bay inside the sphere.

Remember was calling them to her.

"We don't have to go, you know."

"I'm not keen on starving to death," Grond said, adjusting his bandage, which had fresh bloodstains on it. "We broke her fuckin' rules and now she's calling us to account. I don't see any way this plays out other than to *let it play out*. You think she's just gonna turn the inertia beam off and let us go? I doubt it."

"We could have Rhundi come get us."

Grond glared at him. "You know twelve reasons that won't work and I'm not going to bother explaining them to you. Only decision we actually get to make here is what we're doing with Ilana."

"May as well take her with us," Brazel said. "She'll get to tell everybody she met Remember. That's gotta be worth something."

"Assuming she doesn't take her out too," Grond said. "Another body on our conscience. All right. Go get her. Meet me outside."

Brazel made his way to the cargo hold, collecting Ilana's confiscated weapons along the way. She was pacing the hold, muttering to herself.

He tossed her the weapons. "We're stuck, and the two of us have to take a little trip. You're not going to be able to go anywhere until we get back, and for all I know we might not be coming back. So you can wait here and take your chances that eventually you'll be able to take the ship or you can come with us and see what happens. Your call."

"What the hell was that?" She had an angry bruise on the side of her face; she had clearly taken a hard hit when the ship was pulled out of tunnelspace.

"We made somebody mad. She's requested an interview, and she didn't do it in the nicest possible way. You ever heard of Lady Remember?"

A strange look crossed her face.

"Yeah. You're ... you're tangled up with Remember? And you're going to see her now?"

"Quite possibly for her to kill us, yes."

"I'm in," she said. "Always up to meet a celebrity."

"Hopefully that's not the worst mistake you ever made," he said. "If it is, it'll be your last."

Brazel filled Ilana in on the finer points of instantaneous intergalactic transport— and the distinct possibility that she would wake up naked with two relatively unfamiliar, and also naked, men— on the way into the teleporter room in the center of the sphere. "You're not going to have your guns, either, so hope that she plans on sending you back," he added. Neither of them had bothered to bring anything of any importance with them this time, assuming that the teleporter would simply leave it behind again.

There were *three* glasses of the odd blue drink sitting on the threshold of the teleporter.

"Well, okay," Brazel said, drinking his. "So much for surprising her."

A few minutes later, Ilana weaving a bit unsteadily, they were in the lobby. This time, there were two floating 'bots along with their robes, which were again neatly wrapped in ribboned packages. Both were armed.

"Please come this way," one of them said. "Lady Remember will be with you shortly."

Brazel glanced over at his partner. The teleporter had even left his bandage behind; Grond's scar was roughly stitched together. It wasn't good enough to be medbot work; he'd done it himself. Brazel winced. *That must have hurt.* He absentmindedly tucked the ribbon from the package into his pocket again.

"We go nowhere," Grond said, putting his robe on. "Remember meets with us personally, and she meets with us *here*. We're not taking another fucking step."

The two 'bots leveled their guns at Grond.

"I think Remember knows she's going to need to send more than two," Grond said offhandedly. The big halfogre didn't look the slightest bit intimidated.

"I'm not with these guys," Ilana said, casually moving away from Grond and Brazel.

There was a brief, tense moment of silence.

The 'bots folded their guns away.

"The lady Remember agrees to meet with you in person," one of them said. "But you will come with us nonetheless."

Grond and Brazel exchanged a look.

"Good enough," Grond said. "Lead the way."

They were taken a different way this time, not to the library but to a simple room, wood-paneled, with a large table with seats for half a dozen and another fireplace. Grond sat in one by the door, putting his feet up on the table. Brazel and Ilana circled around, putting themselves closer to the fire.

Remember arrived a moment later, the door swinging open without announcement and seemingly on its own. In the flesh she looked much like her flaming avatar had before. Her hair was white, tied in a loose topknot that fell to below her waist. Her clothes were loose, flowing, covering most of her flesh; only her hands and her face showed, and she still had her hands clasped behind her back. Her skin was lined, caramel-colored, papery like an old woman's, but none of an old woman's frailty showed in the rest of her.

The form underneath the robes looked robust and strong.

"You did not follow your instructions," Remember said.

That was as far as she got. There was a wet, meaty *tearing* sound from the front of the room and Grond leapt at Remember, his narrow shiv in his hand, his arm freely bleeding again. The halfogre went for Remember's neck with the blade, and Remember ... just suddenly *wasn't there* any more. Brazel had never seen a dodge so elegant; she had slid around Grond like she was made of smoke, forcing the halfogre to pivot and try again. Almost faster than Brazel could see, Grond took three, four, *five* swings with the blade at Remember, all of them narrowly missing their mark. Remember had a broad grin on her face, a weird silvery tint starting to take over in her eyes.

She never moved her hands from behind her back.

Brazel felt something cold and hard pressing into the back of his neck. He glanced to his right.

"Grond."

The halfogre ignored him, red-eyed and roaring now, trying his best to lay even a single *finger* on Remember and failing.

"Grond."

Something in Brazel's tone got through this time, and the halfogre hesitated, holding the blade in front of him, amazingly *out of breath*. Brazel had seen the halfogre in battles hours long; seeing him winded was incredibly rare.

Ilana had a gun to the back of Brazel's head. A gun that she certainly *hadn't* had after the teleporter; there hadn't really been anywhere for her to hide one. Which meant it was either in the box with her robe or in the room, waiting for her. Which meant she was one of Remember's people.

Which meant she was fair game. Brazel had learned many years ago that most humans had no real idea how to hold a gnome at gunpoint; the height difference never worked in their favor. He dropped to the floor in a flash, simultaneously shoving her gun hand high, over his head and toward Remember. He scuttled between her legs and climbed up onto her back, yanking the ribbon from his robe out of his pocket and wrapping it twice around her neck, squeezing tightly. Ilana slumped to the floor, unable to bear his weight on her back, scrabbling at the improvised garrote and dropping her gun.

"Okay, you're a badass, and Grond can't hurt you," he said. "I can hurt *her*. Your move."

The grin on Remember's face *broadened*, if anything. She cast a sidelong glance at Grond, straightened herself up, and bowed to the two of them.

"I said you had not followed directions. I was given no opportunity to discuss my opinion of your transgressions. You may release my employee; you are in no danger."

Brazel grabbed Ilana's gun from the floor and hit her in the back of the head, knocking her unconscious.

"Only lady gets to hold me at gunpoint is my wife," he said. "I tend to take it personally."

Remember watched her fall to the floor and shrugged.

"I would appreciate it if you would put down the knife," she said.

Grond slammed the knife into the table, snapping it in half.

"You're responsible for *eighty thousand dead*," he growled. "And you brought *us* into it."

"Untrue," Remember said. "It is not outside the realm of possibility that *she*," this with a nod at Ilana, "is partially responsible, but you are not. The disease had begun to spread before you even landed."

"So you sent us into a plague zone without any warning? That's *not* better," Brazel retorted. "I went home to my *wife and kids* after that job."

"You had no risk of infection," Remember said. "The liquid you imbibed prior to the delivery saw to that. A simple nanoinhibitor. One that could be manufactured in high quantities, given the right equipment."

"The box," Brazel said. "Is *that* what the damn thing was for? You were trying to cure the plague? But the plague took over the planet anyway."

"It didn't work," Remember said, shrugging. "I had hoped to arrest the plague, or even stop it in its tracks, but I failed. The cure worked on you, however. It is apparently more effective when ingested."

"Why the hell didn't you *tell* us?" Grond said, his eyes still shining red, although most of the aggression had gone out of his stance. "You knew this was going to happen and you sent us in anyway?"

"I told you that I would be monitoring you to see how well you followed your instructions," Remember said calmly. "I said nothing about whether I *expected you* to follow those instructions. If the cure had worked, the twenty-five day cycle would have been sufficient to clear the nanovirus from the surrounding area. If you had not returned once news of the plague became public, I would know you to be cowards; men of little conviction or moral strength. You returned to save people, against my clear instructions, with no thought to the consequences."

"*Plenty* of thought to the consequences," Brazel corrected.

Remember smiled again. "But you did it anyway."

"And the girl?"

"Insurance," Remember replied. "She was to try to arrest the disease at its source more ... directly than you were told to. She failed as well. It seems that some things ... cannot be changed, after all."

"The medical firm on the top floor," Grond said. "They set the plague loose?"

"Unwittingly, I believe," Remember said. "Intent so rarely matters, unfortunately."

"You're lying," Grond said. "Or deliberately concealing something. How the hell did you even know about the plague in time to send us there to stop it?"

"Some things I will not be sharing with you," Remember said, a hint of ice creeping into her voice. "Learn to live with ambiguity."

No one said anything for a moment.

"You have two choices before you," Remember said. "The first is to choose to believe me, or not, and accept your payment and the likelihood that I will be using your services in the future. The second is to choose to try to kill me again. You will find that this time I will not restrain myself." Her hands, Brazel noticed, had still not moved from behind her back.

Brazel looked at Grond. The halfogre shrugged, clearly still angry but accepting the inevitable.

"We'll take that payment now," he said.

"A word on that," Remember said. "I offered you a certain sum for following my instructions. You did not follow those instructions. And there is a small matter of some destroyed property as well," glancing at Grond.

"You're trying to welsh?" Brazel asked.

"I am not *trying* anything," Remember said. "I have altered the deal. You will find, however, that the end result will still be to your liking. Your wife owns a partial stake in a resort on Arradon, yes?"

Brazel nodded, feeling the blood drain out of his face. *This can't be good.*

"You will find that she now owns the *entire* resort," Remember continued. "With my compliments. Her network of informants is ... impressive. Even to me."

Brazel ran the numbers in his head. Their pay had been cut by about a third, but Rhundi would be able to turn her stake in the resort into much more money in no time, and she'd been trying to buy her partners out for *years* without success.

"Grond?"

The halfogre nodded.

"Fine," Brazel said.

"I will be in touch when I require you again," Remember said, turning to leave.

"And what if we want *you*?" Grond asked.

Remember paused.

"You will find," she said, "that the two events will tend to overlap. Look for the *Memento*."

She left the room, her robe trailing behind her. The door swung open to admit her, then closed.

"What memento does she want us to look for? Awful cryptic," Brazel said.

"It's a goddamn pun," Grond said. "It's the name of the teleporter."

Brazel thought about it for a moment. "I'm not sure I get it."

"A memento is an object," Grond said. "One that leads you to remember."

Brazel snickered.

"C'mon, let's go," he said. "I'll let you be the one who gets to tell Rhundi about her new resort, what with the old woman beating you in a fight and all."

"Bet I can hit *you*," Grond responded.

"Let's get out of here first," Brazel said. "You can try and hit me all you want once I'm back in my own ship."

Grond gestured at Ilana, still unconscious on the floor. "Think we should just leave her there?"

"Yeah," Brazel said. "I didn't get the feeling Remember was too happy with her. And I think that's two she owes us, now."

"Works for me," Grond said, following his partner out of the room.

⋊⟨⊡⟩⋉

"THE CONTRACT"

"Explain to me exactly why this has to be my problem."

The goblin wrung her hands, stress evident on her face, her fur and ears held flat. "We can't make him go away, ma'am. He says he has a contract. He's not scared of us. Maybe you send Grond?"

Rhundi raised an eyebrow, letting her own fur raise up a bit in response. Her husband Brazel and his halfogre partner were a couple parsecs away; they were finished with their job, but she'd just told Brazel about a delivery job that had come up. They'd likely be taking care of that before they came home, which meant they were probably not going to be back for a few days at the very earliest.

Not that anyone else really needed to know that.

"You're not suggesting I can't handle this on my own."

The goblin deflated further, staring at the ground and continuing to rub her hands together. "No, ma'am. Of course not. Just that— well, you're the boss. You shouldn't have to, ma'am."

Rhundi ignored that.

"Did he show you the contract?"

"He says the contract says he doesn't have to, ma'am. He wouldn't even open the door. He doesn't anymore, unless we've brought meals, and then only after we leave."

"I own the place. He doesn't have a contract that says he doesn't have to show it to me."

The goblin cringed again, saying nothing.

Rhundi rubbed her forehead. She had only just recently assumed full control of the resort, and it had become abundantly clear to her quickly that previous management had made frequent poor decisions regarding their treatment of the staff. "It's not your fault... what was your name again?"

"We are Corvix clan, ma'am. This one is Twelve." Goblins were strongly group-oriented; personal names were perceived as being for family only. There were thirty-seven goblins working at the resort, none of whom would divulge their personal names. She apparently had at least twelve members of the Corvix clan on staff.

Rhundi nodded. "Twelfth Corvix, you are not to blame for this. I will deal with him. You may return to work." The goblin nodded and scurried out of Rhundi's office.

She pushed a button on her desk console, opening a comm to her personal secretary.

"Gorrim."

"Yes, ma'am." Gorrim had an unusually deep voice for a gnome, and it sounded odd to hear him through the desk comm.

"Call the troll. Tell him I'm coming to see him in an hour, and tell him if he tries to lock me out this time I'm going to take the door down. If he says a single thing about a contract, tell him I'm bringing Grond with me."

"He's not going to like that, ma'am."

"I'm not going to like it either. Do it anyway."

She cut the connection.

Rhundi's resort— she was renaming the place, now that she owned it, but hadn't come up with a suitably grand name for it yet— was, at the most, a mid-level tourist attraction on the planet of Arradon, a smallish rock in one of the more out-of-the-way tentacles of gnomespace. Owing to some quirks of planetary geography and location, the entire planet was regarded as a tourist destination by most of the galaxy, so she had her work cut out for her if she intended to make a name for herself in legitimate work. She'd started off as a jack-of-all-trades, much like her husband— it sounded nicer than "smuggler" or "fence," which were a bit more accurate— but she'd been trying to steadily increase the amount of capital their family was able to accumulate from more legitimate work. She'd owned a third of the resort only a few months ago; both of her business partners had abruptly sold their shares to her on very little notice and vacated the planet altogether. She had her suspicions as to their reasons but had been too busy to look into them. There was too much to do.

The troll on the fifth level was one of the problems she'd managed to inherit. Large portions of the resort were subterranean; she wanted to expand, and she was going to have to demolish the suite of rooms he occupied in order to do it. He had occupied them for nearly fifteen years.

And he was not terribly interested in moving.

In general, the resort did not cater to long-term stays; most of their guests were on-planet for no more than a few weeks. The troll's rent had been changed any number of times without complaint; he appeared to be independently wealthy and, apparently, working from home, as he rarely left his rooms, having his meals— the same meals, every day— brought to him by the staff. He hadn't been difficult, really; in fact, he had made her an awful lot of money over the years. But he was in the way of her making more money, and that meant he needed to move.

There were any number of ways to handle the situation; all of the gentle ones short of her showing up had been used. The next step after a personal conference would involve lawyers, subterfuge, or force, none of which she was terribly interested in at the moment. No, she'd have to visit him herself.

She walked to the troll's suite. There were lifts and personal transports that could have gotten her there faster; she wanted the time to think, and it was good for her employees to see her out and about in the resort instead of stuck in her office. She noted fourteen things that needed her attention along the way, memorizing a mental list as she walked. The entryway to the troll's suite was the fifteenth; you could tell you were underground while walking down the final corridor to his door. It was damp and cold, as if the climate balancers weren't reaching it properly, and the approach lacked artistry as well. He was in one of her larger suites; the bare, straight corridor to his door was not up to the degree of decor and class that she expected from what was now her own establishment.

She stood in front of the door, letting the suite security scan her. Every resident had the right to set rules for who could bother them; the door was soundproofed enough that knocking would do no good. If the guest was interested enough in privacy it would take a small explosion outside their rooms for them to notice it inside. She had an override, of course, as did most of the staff, and the suite would be telling the troll that she was standing outside in moments. If he didn't let her in, she'd let herself in.

She gave him three minutes, counting the heartbeats.

Nothing happened.

"Open," she said. "Authorize override Rhundi Tavh're'muil. Password *Darsi*." Darsi was her and Brazel's firstborn. It wasn't the most secure password in existence, but the voiceprint and bioscan were proof enough of her identity without it.

Nothing continued to happen.

"You've *got* to be fucking kidding," she said. The damn troll had hacked her security software. Well, he hadn't replaced the door. She'd brought a gun. She pulled it out and aimed it at the latch.

Wait.

She reached out and put her hand on the door; gave it an experimental push. The door didn't give at all. Almost all of the standard doors across the resort were hollow-core but filled with soundproofing gel. There should have been just the tiniest amount of give when she shoved on it.

"You *have* replaced the door, you clever bastard," she said.

She took a moment to think.

"Sirrys ban Irtuus bon Alaamac," she said, using the troll's threefold, formal name. "I know you are inside and I know you do not wish visitors. I also know that you can hear me. I intend to get inside your room. It is best for both of us if this happens peacefully. If I must force my way inside it will not go well for you." She was going to have to figure out how to get a tunnel 'bot into this corridor anyway to widen it; she couldn't imagine a single thing the troll could have rigged inside his suite that would keep that out. The things were designed for digging through bedrock, and the widened access would be considerably broader than his doorway anyway.

"You have three minutes," she said, counting heartbeats again.

She heard the door click unlocked in two minutes and fifty-six seconds.

Smug bastard, she thought. He hadn't bothered to actually open the thing; he'd just unlocked it. She opened the door herself and stepped through.

It was immediately apparent that the troll hadn't let housekeeping in in a very, very long time. The smell of poorly-washed troll, as well as rotten odors of old food and some sort of weird chemical and ozone mix, was so thick it was nearly physically crawling into her snout— and gnomes had exceptionally acute senses of smell— an evolutionary perk that she found herself regretting.

She ignored it. The room was going to be demolished; the smell didn't matter.

Sirrys ban Irtuus bon Alaamac stood before her. Well, slightly *below* her, technically; trolls had a remarkably malleable physiology and could go from shorter than a gnome but broader than a dwarf to cadaverously thin but taller than an ogre in a matter of seconds. This troll was scarcely a meter tall at the moment but was actually wider than he was tall; his bluish skin sagged off his body and gathered into rolls at his joints and hips. He had a long, narrow nose and a pointed chin that contrasted sharply with his saggy voluminosity everywhere else, and a shock of stiff straw-colored hair that spread from the top of his head down his back and over his shoulders. In troll style, he wore a loose lower garment gathered at his waist and nothing else on his upper body. It was difficult to design clothing that elongated and contracted with a troll's upper body, so they often didn't bother. Pants were simply easier.

"I have a *contract*," the troll whined.

"It honors me that you do not pretend you don't know why I'm here," Rhundi replied. "Your contract is not with me. It is not even with the owners immediately prior to me. And you've never actually shown it to me."

"It is not to be shown to you," the troll said, this time in a slightly less plaintive tone of voice.

"I have no idea what that means, Sirrys ban Irtuus—"

"Call me Irtuus-bon," the troll said, his mood— and his size— shifting abruptly. "Come." He turned on a heel and stalked off, his body lengthening as he walked. Rhundi took a moment to look around. She'd entered into a sitting room; the lights had been switched out for something darker; the troll's eyes likely worked on a slightly different set of wavelengths from hers. The room looked nearly unused; there was dust on the furniture and the floor, but a clean path from the door to the room that Irtuus-bon— now at his full height— had disappeared into. She spent a moment considering the possibility that the troll had lived in this suite for fifteen years and had never once sat down in the front room.

That possibility became a certainty the moment she followed him. The troll led her into one of the bedrooms. These were generally all furnished in similar fashion; one oversized or two smaller beds, a couple of desks, a couple of dressers, a large mirror, and one to three seats of varying degrees of softness for sitting or reclining. There was a cot in a corner of the room. The rest of it was dedicated to computer equipment; an entire wall had been given over to an enormous monitor displaying several dozen data readouts and a handful of maps, simultaneously.

Her first thought, ridiculously, was *how did we not notice the power drain?*

Her second thought was to wonder where the enormous hole in the wall opposite her led to. It wasn't supposed to be there, and the troll had never bothered to finish his renovations. There was simply a large hole dug through the wall and into what was supposed to be bedrock behind it. The damn troll had *expanded his living space*. Her partners had either never known about it or simply hadn't bothered to inform her of it.

Mental note: deal with extreme rage issues later.

She followed the troll into his hole, going down a half-flight of stairs into the cavern he'd somehow managed to open behind his apartment. It looked as if at least part of it was natural, but over the years he'd reinforced the roof and managed to power and light the entire thing. There were more computer consoles and wall monitors all around the space, which was roughly circular and perhaps ten meters wide, with a five-meter ceiling, more than high enough for an ogre or a troll at his tallest to feel perfectly comfortable. A hollow in the wall led to yet another cavern beyond theirs.

Irtuus-bon stood in the center of the room, next to a holomap that had to have cost a sizeable portion of Rhundi's annual income. He pushed a button and the thing burst into live, spreading a map of what looked like most of known space across the room. Bits of it were shaded red, glowing. Benevolence space.

"What do you know of the Benevolence?" he asked.

Rhundi went cold. This couldn't be a setup. He'd been there far too long for that to be possible, living right under her nose. It *couldn't* be a setup.

"Only what everyone knows," she said. "They don't bother us out here, so we get along fine."

"Sssss ..." the troll answered. "A most ... *political* response. You are cautious. This is good. I know what you are, Rhundi Tavh're'muil, and I know what your husband and his most interesting halfogre partner are as well. I have known for ... a long time ... and I have not betrayed you yet. I will not be starting tonight. But, as you can see, I cannot acquiesce to your desire that I relocate, either."

She took a moment to take this all in. Brazel and Grond's activities were hardly a carefully guarded secret but she hadn't thought they'd ever been clear to the tenants before.

Focus on the important parts, she thought. *Figure out the rest later.*

"What have you been doing here?" she asked.

"This way," he beckoned, and disappeared into the hollow.

Rhundi adjusted her gun and followed.

The chamber the troll led her into was even larger than the one they'd left. Again, it looked as if Irtuus-bon had enlarged and reinforced a natural cavity in the rock. This one, however, contained no technology beyond that needed to light the room. This room contained artifacts. Hundreds of them, on shelves built into the wall and freestanding shelves and tables scattered around. Some of the objects were stone or wood or bone; others were made of materials harder to recognize. Many of them bore clear symbols or sigils etched or painted on them. One caught Rhundi's eye; there was a section near her devoted to dozens of symbols that bore a faint resemblance to an insect, an eight-legged monstrosity with one central eye.

"Do you recognize these?" the troll said.

Rhundi looked around, trying to find anything familiar.

"I do not," she said.

He brought her a ruined, broken piece of alloy; whatever the material was they made the outer hulls of ships from.. The spider symbol was painted on it--

hurriedly, it seemed, as it had dripped in places before it dried.

"This, perhaps?"

"It's a piece of metal," she said. "Wreckage, or salvage. It could have come from anything."

"From a ship, in fact," he said. "A ship you knew very well."

Rhundi let her lip curl derisively.

"You can't possibly be serious." It was part of a ship, and the paint job, though pitted and scratched, was the right color, but--

"Ah, so you do know it," the troll replied.

"This is not a piece of the *Incandescent*," Rhundi insisted calmly. "That ship was blown to bits half a lifetime ago, practically on the other side of the galaxy. Just because it's the right goddamn color doesn't make it the same ship. You're not fooling me, Irtuus-bon." Her hand drifted toward her gun again. What was his game? Just to rattle her? This was too stupid to work. She was better at that than the troll was. She'd rattled with the best of them.

"I collect things," the troll said, ignoring her. "Sometimes people bring me interesting things, or send them to me, and sometimes I hear of events and I make requests. You know the Benevolence; better than you have admitted to me. You know of them better than most do, in fact. But not better than I; no, not at all. I know the Benevolence, and I know their magic, and I know their *gods*, Rhundi Tavh're'muil. Each of these artifacts is a story; some of death, some of rebirth, some of stranger things. Your ship was not destroyed by accident. It was cursed. This symbol is the proof."

"Anyone could have painted that on the wreckage afterwards. And I'm far from convinced that it's even a piece of my ship."

"Believe what you will," the troll said. "I say this to you: the Benevolence do believe. And their beliefs have been known to ... change things."

She blinked. *I've let him change the subject*, she thought.

"You haven't actually answered me," she said. "Although I appreciate the attempt to distract me with superstitious nonsense. I'll not ask a third time, Irtuus-bon: what are you doing at my resort?"

His mood changed again, and he lost half of his height in an eyeblink. He cackled. "Clever, you are, so clever. Sirrys ban Irtuus bon Alaamac is proud. Shall I give you the truth, this time?"

"I believe you have given me some of the truth already," she said. "But not enough."

"More, then," he said.

"More. My patience is growing short. I would not like this to end impolitely."

He cackled again, staring at her. She returned the stare, impassive. He turned away, stomping out of the room. She followed to find him rummaging through a pile of data pads. He produced one for her. It looked as if he had had it for some time.

"My contract," he said.

She powered it on and scrolled through. It didn't take long; it wasn't especially complicated.

"This entitles you to a long-term lease," she said. "There is no mention of this particular suite, no mention of any conditions that prevent me from entering, and-- rather importantly-- absolutely nothing that entitles you to carve holes in my walls or run an unauthorized ... whatever all *this* is."

"Old owners never looked," he said. "Fooled them."

"I think I want Irtuus-bon back," she said. "I liked him more."

The troll blinked a couple of times, shrugged, and grew.

"Your other incarnations are rather childish," Rhundi said.

"As must they be," Irtuus-bon replied. "My people contain multitudes."

"My people are somewhat more straightforward. You will reveal to me in simple language what you have been doing in this room for all these years, with no subterfuge or misdirection, and you will do it now, or I will forcibly evict you and turn these things you're harboring over to the Benevolence."

The troll's eyes narrowed. "Sss. Overplaying your hand, I think. You would not... willingly draw the attention of Benevolence, not out here. There are very good reasons I chose your planet to do my work; the disinclination of the Benevolence to come anywhere near it is a large portion of those reasons."

Rhundi reached for her gun, and the troll raised a hand, continuing. "I do, however, believe the threat of force. I am a researcher and a collector and a historian. I watch the Benevolence, Rhundi Tavh're'muil. I collect their scraps when they come into my possession and I collect knowledge of their movements from ... well, everywhere I can. Trolls, as it turns out, are exceptionally good at this sort of thing. It may be that we are not taken as seriously by the Benevolence as perhaps we should."

"Tell me something I don't know."

"Would the current location of the *Testament* be sufficient?"

Oh my. The *Testament* was the Benevolence's flagship. There were any number of reasons why having a handle on its location might be useful.

"It would, if you could prove it."

Irtuus-bon sighed. "Well, you could go to it and see, but by then it would likely be elsewhere."

"Try again, then."

"You have in your possession a suit of Benevolence armor and some of their weaponry, yes?"

No use denying it. "I do." She'd thought about trying to move the items, but had held on to them instead. You never knew when something like that might come in handy.

"And you have had no luck in getting their weapons to fire."

"Also correct." Grond had gotten curious one day and had taken one of the rifles out for some target practice. He'd come back frustrated, the rifle nearly entirely disassembled, with no clue what was preventing it from firing. "These are, however, things that I know. I believe I specified the opposite."

"I am about to hand you a weapon. Do not panic." The troll stretched to his full height, reaching behind one of the displays mounted on the wall. He revealed a Benevolence rifle, a near-identical model to the ones that Grond and Brazel had brought back to her.

"I would ask that you not fire this in my room," he said, "but you should be able to verify that it will. Use … a light touch on the trigger." He held out the weapon to her, butt-first, taking care to never point the business end of the thing at her. In fact, he was keeping it pointed at his own chest.

Rhundi stifled back a snort. She'd been handling weapons since before she could swim; she wasn't about to accidentally fire any Benevolence hardware in her own place no matter how much she wanted to renovate. She applied the barest touch of pressure to the trigger and felt the gun warm up to her touch. Benevolence weaponry, like most weapons that fired energy instead of projectiles, generated ammunition as the trigger was pulled. She could feel the subtle vibrations of the thing starting to warm up and could smell the tell-tale, burnt-ozone scent that it produced. The gun would work. Grond hadn't even been able to get his trigger to move.

"How?"

"A combination of a number of things," the troll replied, "all of which I will be happy to share with you once the matter of my rooms is settled. Needless to say, I can convert most of their weaponry to general use, at least in theory. Actual working examples to test are … sss … as you might imagine, somewhat difficult to come by."

"I cannot allow you to remain here," Rhundi replied. "That is not negotiable. You are moving."

A sudden movement on his part, as the troll tried to snatch the rifle away and reverse it. He counted on his greater strength to help him. It proved less than useful, as Rhundi simply let her feet leave the ground and let the troll's own movement pull her off the ground and into his body. She wrapped a hand around his neck-- which was, at the moment, thin-- and scrambled onto his back, her gun pressed firmly against his temple.

"That was foolish," she said. "If your neck starts feeling too thick for me to break easily, you can expect me to start shooting. Get on your knees. Now."

Irtuus-bon complied.

"Drop the rifle. In fact, toss it across the room."

He followed those instructions as well.

"Now stretch out on the floor, hands over your head and flat on the ground."

A moment of shuffling on the troll's part left her perched on his back with him flat on the ground and his hands in a safe position. Her gun remained at the back of his head.

"You said I overreached earlier, Irtuus-bon. You were probably right. But understand that I am *not* bluffing now. I am, in fact, offering you a *deal*. You can accept it, you can leave my property *right now*, forever, with none of your belongings, or you can make anything *remotely* like a sudden movement and I can blow your head clear off of your shoulders. Tap your finger on the ground *once* if you would like to hear my proposal or *twice* if you would like to leave under armed escort. Anything else, including three taps, and I start shooting. And I *assure you* I am faster than you are."

He hesitated for a moment, then tapped a long finger once on the floor.

"You *are* moving.   I want this space for expansion, and now that you've gone to the trouble of locating a cave network down here that will make my expansion *easier*, there's no way I'm backing off on those plans. That doesn't mean that you are *leaving*. In fact, I plan to relocate you somewhere *better*. Closer to me, in fact, where you won't have to run illicit power lines and I can keep an eye on you. Whatever you're currently stealing from me to run your operation, I'll provide. And your rent? Consider your living expenses your *pay* now. But everything you discover and everything you know? Is *mine* in exchange."

She paused for a moment, letting him take this in.

"That's your deal, Irtuus-bon. You give up your gross, dusty hole in the ground and your bootleg, cobbled-together equipment for a dedicated power source and the best stuff I can buy. And your days as a freelancer are over. It's that, homelessness, or a hole in the one part of your body that you can't *shrink*. You have ten seconds to think about it. Tap once if you agree."

She let thirty seconds go by before giving a slight nudge to the back of the troll's head with the gun.

He tapped once. She let herself breathe.

"I'm going to back up now. So are you. You are going to do *nothing stupid* and you are not going to stand up any shorter or more obnoxious than you are right now."

She took a few steps back, toward the rifle, keeping herself in between it and Irtuus-bon. The troll slowly pulled himself to his feet, stretching his joints. He had, surprisingly, a gleam in his eyes that almost looked like happiness.

"I'm keeping the rifle," she said. "Anything else dangerous in here that I should know about?"

"Some of the artifacts could be *incredibly* so," he replied.

She considered this. "Anything in there you can shoot me with?"

"Not that kind of dangerous," he admitted.

"I'll be back in a day," she said. "In between now and then, I want you to make me a wish list. Let me know what you need and how much you think it will cost. I'll let you know after I see it how much of it I think you're going to *get*. Do we have a deal?"

"We ... sss ... have a *deal*," the troll responded. Yes, that was definitely happiness, no matter how much he was trying to hide it.

"Good," she said, pivoting on one heel and walking out of the room. "And that door had better let me in the next time I come back, too."

She let the door shut behind her as she left, wrinkling her nose again at the damp smell in the outer corridor. No wonder; there were unventilated cave systems attached directly to the room. It was a wonder she hadn't had mold problems.

At least I didn't need any lawyers, she thought. *It could have gone worse.*

⊰⊡⊱

"SIGIL"

"There's a job," Brazel said.

"We're on a job right now," Grond replied. "There can't be another job until the first job is finished."

"Technically, we're on our way *back* from a job," Brazel answered, nonchalantly smoothing his fur. "The job itself is finished. The only bits left are delivery and receiving of payment, and we've got a solid week before deadline. That's plenty of time for a side trip."

Grond pointed at his ear. Both of his ears were masses of scar tissue under the best of circumstances, but one of them looked rather more singed than usual.

"That'll heal," Brazel said.

"It'll heal with time," Grond growled, "and some time is exactly what I was looking forward to just now. Time, and a book. Maybe a cold compress or two."

"Speaking of that," Brazel said, making sure he was comfortably out of his halfogre partner's rather long reach. "Keeping it cold won't be hard."

Grond's eyes flashed red.

"No," he said.

"It's a *little* ice planet," Brazel said.

"NO," Grond said again, putting a bit more bass into his voice this time. "No ice planets. I told you no ice planets. You know this."

"They're not that bad," Brazel whined.

"You are a *gnome*. You have *fur*," Grond said. "I do not. You're fucking adapted to living on an ice planet. Ogres live on planets with jungles and deserts. Not on damned iceballs."

"There's a penalty rider in the contract," Brazel said. "We get an extra twenty percent if the temperature goes under fifty below." He spent most of the next thirty seconds dodging, as Grond threw a few convenient heavy objects at him.

"I'm taking sixty percent of the fee," Grond said. "You know I hate ice planets."

"I worked that into the bargaining," Brazel answered. This was not precisely true; his wife Rhundi had done all of the legwork on this contract, but she knew Grond's preferences as well as Brazel did, and had pushed hard to make the job worth the pay. "It's a milk run anyway. The planet's in dwarfspace. We pick up a package from somebody and we deliver it to-- get this-- anywhere outside of dwarfspace. And then we get paid."

This was unexpected. Grond paused for a moment, thinking.

"You know what the package is, right?" he said.

"Person in a box, obviously," Brazel answered. "I'm guessing a dwarfcicle of some sort who's trying to flee, so probably a male." It would not be the first time they'd been asked to quietly spirit someone out of dwarfspace; in fact, it nearly counted as a full-blown side racket for them.

"Why not hide it a little bit?" Grond said. "What other possible reason would we have to just deliver outside of dwarfspace? There's really not even a planet or a system to take it to? Just 'anywhere'?"

"Anywhere," Brazel said. "And that means that our contract is probably with the dwarf himself. Rhundi said the job came through a whole complicated network of fronts; she hadn't sorted through everything yet but had a feeling it was legit."

"You're sending me to an ice planet to pick up what is probably a dwarfcicle in a box based on a *feeling* that it's not going to get us killed," the halfogre said. "Do you think that makes me any happier than I was before?"

Brazel said a number. The halfogre's eyes lost their red sheen and widened slightly.

"Now *that* makes me feel better," Grond said. "But you'd better not bitch about it the next time I send you to Kratuul."

The gnome shrugged. They could have that argument later.

"The planet's only half a day off," he said. "Barely even counts as a course correction. We'll be in and out in no time."

"Find a way to make it quicker," the halfogre said. "And there had damn well better be some cold-weather gear stowed on this boat someplace."

⊰⊚⊱

The planet, in true dwarven fashion, was named only with numbers; the dwarves called it 00901213. It was, as Grond had feared, an ice planet, far enough from its star that it would only barely register as a sun from the planet's surface. It was tiny, too, but despite being smaller than many actual moons that Grond and Brazel had walked upon, it had two of its own: captured nickel-iron asteroids, from the look of them, each about a dozen or so kilometers wide, that whirled around the planet in a day or two each.

"We shall call it *Shithole*," Grond said, looking at a holo of the planet.

"Do the moons get names?" Brazel asked.

"Nah. Fuck 'em for not choosing a better planet to orbit," Grond said. "How much do we need to know about this place?"

Brazel shrugged. "No major population centers; the package is at what appears to be either a hermitage or a small research station. There's some mining, but it's on the opposite side of the rock from where we're going; basically a few pockets of heavy industry among a whole lot of nothing. Shithole's too small to have much of an atmosphere, so we'll need envirosuits with a supply until we can get into somewhere pressurized."

"We needed envirosuits anyway," Grond said.

"Right, I completely forgot it was cold on account of you hadn't whined about it in ten minutes," Brazel retorted. "Point is, you won't be able to breathe enough useful air into your lungs to complain during the couple of minutes it'll take you to freeze to death. Our target is actually mostly underground, not a domed hab like most of the surface structures-- it's apparently actually accessed through the side of a mountain, believe it or not."

"Do they know we're coming?"

"Apparently," the gnome said. "Which doesn't quite square with the dwarfcicle idea. But there's a place to land almost on top of the doorway, so we won't have to travel too much to get where we're going. You'll barely be outside at all. And even if they weren't, Namey hasn't spotted anything that looks like planetary defenses. The rock's harmless." Namey was Brazel's nickname for their ship, the *Nameless*. He and Grond had argued for months about what to name the boat when they bought it, and had never settled on an acceptable answer.

"Dwarven research station, I assume."

"Yeah, so probably not sized for bigs. But we won't be there long."

Grond shrugged. At 2.4 meters tall, he was nearly twice his partner's size, but he had spent most of his adult life in the company of gnomes, and was well used to existing in places that didn't cater to beings his size. So long as the ceilings were manageable-- and dwarves were taller than gnomes, so they ought to be-- he would be fine.

"So long as there's no complications," Grond said.

"I wish you hadn't said that," Brazel responded.

NO ANSWER TO OUR HAIL, Namey chirped in.

"That's your fault," Brazel said.

Grond just glared.

"I told you I hate ice planets," he said.

⋊⟨▭⟩⋉

An argument ensued, and by the time it was resolved that they were going to land and check out the station, Namey had, without consulting either of them about it, landed himself on a strip of level ground half a klick away from their target. It really was built into the side of a mountain— a towering, jagged set of frozen peaks that jutted high from a level plain of ice. Unexpectedly, the mountain was located next to a shallow lake, filled with a mirror-sheened white liquid of unclear composition.

"Any sign of anybody home, Namey?" Brazel asked.

THE BASE IS POWERED, the ship responded. NO LIFE SIGNS, BUT MY SENSORS WILL NOT PENETRATE FAR INTO THE ICE. IF THE BASE IS MOSTLY SUBTERRANEAN THE LACK OF LIFE SIGNS WOULD NOT BE SURPRISING.

"Plays merry hell with the idea that they know we're coming, though," Grond said.

THERE CONTINUES TO BE NO RESPONSE TO HAILING FREQUENCIES, Namey continued. I HAVE TRIED A VARIETY OF COMMON DWARVEN, GNOMIC AND HUMAN FREQUENCIES AS WELL AS A NUMBER TYPICALLY USED BY BENEVOLENCE. THERE APPEARS TO BE NO ONE LOOKING.

"Discouraging," the gnome muttered. "We're going in anyway."

"We're arming ourselves a bit more heavily than we'd planned, though," Grond said. He was already pulling on an envirosuit, to which he had strapped a few energy weapons-- the thin atmosphere made projectile weapons unreliable-- as well as his usual complement of sharp things and Angela, his prized Iklis sniper's longbow.

"You're bringing Angie?" Brazel asked. "We'll be indoors. Not much use for a long-range weapon even if we do end up in trouble."

"I don't trust a single thing about this," said Grond, "and I'm not leaving tools behind on the ship. Plus, she's scary. I like scary."

Brazel nodded.

"Also, if you call her Angie again, I'll throw you in the lake," the halfogre added. "Try me if you think I'm kidding."

One thing was clear: they were going to earn the penalty rider for the temperature. Grond flatly refused to even speculate on what the temperature was, but Brazel put up a readout on the faceplate of his envirosuit that registered the temperature at fully ninety degrees below zero. Luckily for both of them, Shithole's thin atmosphere meant that the wind was not a factor. The surface was, in fact, frighteningly still. Shithole had no indigenous life of any kind, and the quiet was almost maddening. The system's sun was a cold white pinprick far in the distance, providing just enough light to the surface to maneuver around without assistance but not enough to see well. Overhead, one of the planet's two moons tumbled by.

"Faster we move, faster we're done," Grond said, and headed toward the station's entrance. This was a round portal-- gratifyingly, sized for bigs-- set into a recessed part of the base of the mountain. There was a simple access panel set into the ice next to the doorway with a single button. He pushed it, and after a few moments the door obligingly glided out of the way.

"Not much on security, are they?" he said.

"Not sure why they would need to be, I guess," Brazel said. "The thing probably locks when they want it to; it's not like they're going to get a lot of drop-ins way out here." The portal opened into a long tunnel; an intercom system was set into a walled booth just inside, along with controls to re-close the door, which Grond did. Fiddling with the intercom produced no response, although the lights were on.

"Down the hallway?" Brazel asked.

"I assume so," Grond replied. They walked for a few minutes, passing through a second larger portal into what was clearly a reception area, with a long counter against the far wall and a few chairs and tables scattered around. There was no one anywhere to be seen.

"Answers the security question," Grond said, walking behind the reception counter. "They'll let you into that outside hallway to get you out of the cold, but I'm guessing there's no way through that second door unless somebody in here buzzes you through. Or-- hmm." He waved his partner over.

There was what looked like a space for door controls set into the employee side of the counter. They'd been ripped out.

"We got lucky; the door must have been unlocked when whoever wrecked the controls," Grond said. "Otherwise you'd be cutting your way in here."

"You mean we," Brazel said.

"I mean *you*," Grond said, "on account of this would have just become your nonsense side job and I'd be back on the ship waiting for you to come to your senses. Namey, you still hear us?"

I DO, the ship responded.

"Anything moves within two hundred thousand kilometers and I want to know about it," he continued.

THAT INCLUDES THE ORBITS OF BOTH MOONS, the ship responded. I ASSUME YOU DO NOT INCLUDE THOSE IN YOUR REQUEST.

"I don't remember programming you to be a smarmy asshole," Grond said.

BRAZEL DID IT, the ship replied.

"I thought you picked the personality," Brazel said.

"We turn him into something more obsequious the second we get back," Grond said. "Yes, asshole boat, you may ignore the moons. Nothing else, other than the two of us. Got it?"

UNDERSTOOD, the *Nameless* replied.

"I'm going to, just this once, suggest that something has gone wrong, that it is not our business what has gone wrong, and that we should just leave without trying to figure out what it is," Grond continued. "There's no one here with a package, no one answered our hails, and the entire station looks to be abandoned, and abandoned with at least a little bit of prejudice. I think we should leave."

"That's no fun," Brazel said.

"I knew you were going to say that," Grond said.

"Like you haven't said it yourself a hundred times," Brazel retorted. "You just don't like it here because of the climate. I'm perfectly comfortable."

"Or, at least, you would be, if you could breathe the air."

Brazel snickered. "Actually, there's still atmosphere in here. It's probably safe to crack the faceplates if you want."

"I'm good," Grond said. "At least until we have some idea why we're alone."

"Only one way to find out," Brazel said.

The top level of the research station proved to be entirely abandoned-- of living things, if not of furniture and materiel. The rest of the top floor appeared to be devoted to office space, filled with midrange desk consoles and a large server room. The servers were shut down, and a few minutes of experimentation had left Brazel unsuccessful at getting them back online again. Other than the damage to the door controls at reception, there was no sign of vandalism or violence, although the two found a large loading dock that had been left open to the elements, presumably deliberately.

"Do you think anything's missing?" Brazel asked. "Maybe they evacuated or they found something really interesting somewhere and went out to look at it. They're scientists, after all; scientists get curious."

"Doesn't look like it," Grond responded. The dock had a number of six-wheeled ground transports parked in it, but they were prominently numbered and the numbers were consecutive. "I gotta imagine that it'd take a few of these to get everybody out, and if it was some sort of discovery they'd still have left someone behind. And this has been here for at least a couple of days, I think." He dragged a foot across the floor, disturbing some of the dust and snow that had blown in from the open entryway.

"Wait a minute," he said. "Something on the floor."

The two of them spent a few moments sweeping away dust and snow to reveal a large symbol on the floor of the dock. It was black in color, perhaps three meters wide, and more or less in the exact center of the room: an oval shape, with a circle centered inside it, and four curved lines-- two long, two short-- protruding out from each side.

"That look like a spidership to you?"

Brazel squinted. "A little, maybe? It's awfully stylized if it is." Spiderships were the Benevolence's short-range, single-pilot fighter ships. They were basically a metal oval with a viewport in front and eight arms on the sides, which could be used for propulsion, manipulating objects, or precise aiming for weapons. Spiderships' ability to shoot in virtually any direction made them deadly in larger numbers, although the more of their arms they devoted to combat the less maneuverable they became. A typical Benevolence capital ship would have dozens on board, if not more.

Grond squatted, scraping at the symbol with his fingers. "It looks like it's just been painted on, and more hastily than I'd expect from dwarves. It's too sloppy. What's it doing here?"

"No idea. This isn't Benevolence space. And I can't imagine a bunch of dwarven scientists being real big on attracting their attention, either."

"Okay, gnome, you got me. Now I'm curious."

"Oh, sure," Brazel said. "We just found a suggestion that Benevolence are involved with whatever's going on, which means that this thing just went from weird-but-passive to actively dangerous, and now you get interested."

"Let's find an elevator," Grond said. "See how deep this station goes. There have got to be dorms somewhere, at least. If we don't find anything useful, interesting, or expensive in an hour, we'll give up and split."

"Deal," Brazel said.

It didn't take long to locate the lift-- it was in the back of the loading dock, just past where the transports were parked. There was only one other floor for it to go to, and the descent took several minutes. The basement floor was clearly deep below the surface.

The lift glided to a stop. Grond pulled Angela off his back and snapped his wrist, popping her limbs into position, the string crackling with energy. Brazel took a step back, his hand on a gun at his waist.

Nothing happened.

Grond nodded at Brazel, who moved forward to pull the door open. Grond was the better shot and Angela by far a deadlier weapon, so it made more sense for him to have his hands free. Brazel grunted, the heavy doors at first refusing to separate, then catching and sliding apart smoothly.

The doors opened into what was obviously the laboratory/work space of the station. When the station was operational, this would have been bustling with activity; there was equipment and tech everywhere in a large open room, with doors leading to smaller rooms or other labs around the outside.

The station was clearly no longer operational. The entire room had been torn to bits; furniture overturned, equipment smashed, the ashy evidence of small fires everywhere. Most of the lights had been shattered; the few that remained shed a shaky glow over the room. Half of the doors had been torn from their hinges and the remainder were blocked off with rubble and wreckage.

"Bodies?" Brazel asked.

"Don't see any," Grond said.

"Five minutes. Mark."

The two separated quickly, picking their way separately through the room and searching for anyone, living or dead, who could shed some light on what had happened. Grond threw a few larger pieces of equipment out of his way, looking to see if anyone had been buried. Five minutes later, they met in the center of the lab.

"Not a thing," Grond said. "Not a drop of blood, either."

"And somebody did this on purpose," Brazel said. "This isn't an earthquake or a natural disaster. The walls are still standing, everything upstairs is fine.

Somebody-- or a bunch of somebodies-- came down here and did this intentionally."

"Our package?"

"I doubt it, if we were even right about the package being a person. Can you imagine a dwarven male pulling off something like this on his own? It's generally all they can do to summon the willpower and the luck they'd need just to get away from the clans. I've never even heard of one using violence, much less anything on this scale. No, this wasn't dwarves, unless it was a separate clan entirely, and they'd have killed somebody along the way. Where do you think the dorms are?"

"Only two ways to go," Grond said. "Back there through all the shit they've piled up, which will take longer than I like, or back through one of those halls there." He pointed back toward the lift; there were halls stretching in either direction out of the near corners of the larger lab.

"Let's check 'em out," Brazel said.

Grond nodded, taking the lead. The hallway did indeed lead to living space; and living space for the females, at that, judging from the luxury of the furnishings. The hall opened up into what was obviously a common area, with a bar, comfortable chairs and couches and tables, and even a small stage tucked into a corner. A traditional dwarven hearth sat in the middle of the room, directly underneath a ventilation duct to keep smoke and gases from the fire from filling the space. Another corridor to individual rooms continued on past the common room.

The individual dorms were occupied. The pair checked the first three rooms they reached. Each room had either one or two beds, and each bed had a single dwarven female in it. All were either dead or deeply unconscious.

Brazel pulled off a glove and checked for a pulse. "I think she's gone, but it's hard to tell. She's clammy, but ... shit, this could be suspended animation." He pivoted back the faceplate of his helmet and wrinkled his snout, taking a deep sniff of the room. "She doesn't smell dead. I don't smell rot at all, but I don't know if I would in a place like this. There wasn't anything alive on this rock other than the dwarves; I don't know if there's even really enough bacteria around to decompose them properly."

"Look at her hands," Grond said.

The dwarf's knuckles were bloody and bruised. Her clothing was filthy, too, with small rips and tears everywhere.

"Go check a couple more of them," Brazel said, and Grond slipped out of the room silently. The other dwarf in the room was much the same; no clear pulse or signs of life, with the only signs of violence being damage to her hands.

Grond was back in two minutes. "Four more, same stuff. One's got a nice gash on the side of her head but she might have just gotten hit by something while they were ripping their lab apart. And I found this on the floor in one of the rooms." He held out a club that had once been a table leg; it had clearly been ripped from the table and used to pound on things for a while. The business end of the thing was beaten to pieces but there was no blood on it anywhere.

"So they wrecked their own lab," Brazel said. "And they were frenzied enough about it that most of them did it with their bare hands. And then they just came back in here and laid down quietly and died. That's ... ominous." He suddenly felt a strong need to have his envirosuit completely back on, pulling his glove back on, closing his face mask, and double-checking all of his seals; breathing the local air seemed like an incredibly bad idea at the moment.

"I told you I hated ice planets," Grond said.

"You know we've got to check on the males now," Brazel responded.

"Yeah. We do," Grond said.

They abandoned the female wing of the dorms and moved to the males' wing. This was much smaller: rather than an opulent common room, the hallway opened into a barracks, with plain bunks stacked three high set along one wall and simple cubbies along the other for the dwarves' sparse belongings.

There was a pile of bodies in the middle of the room. All had been strangled with identical lengths of black wire.

Neither spoke, moving to the pile and carefully pulling the bodies out, looking for survivors. There were eighteen bodies in all; each one of them was rather unambiguously dead.

Under the pile was a second symbol. This one, rather than having been quickly painted, looked to have been roughly scratched into the floor with something sharp.

"Time to go?" Grond asked.

"Time to go," Brazel confirmed.

The lift was still settled at their floor, and it was all Brazel and Grond could do to keep from running to get back to it. The ride back up felt incredibly slow.

GROND, said the boat.

"We're on our way back," the halfogre responded. "Get warmed up to leave as soon as we get there."

WE HAVE A PROBLEM.

"I do not want to hear about a problem right now."

YOU SAID NOT TO TELL YOU IF THE MOONS WERE MOVING.

"That's right."

I FEEL COMPELLED TO IGNORE THAT ORDER.

"I fucking know the moons are moving, Namey," Grond snapped. "They're orbiting. That's moving. That's what moons do."

I WOULD NOT CHOOSE THE WORD "ORBITING" TO DESCRIBE THE MOTION OF THIS MOON.

Brazel and Grond looked at each other.

"What word would you use?" Brazel asked.

CRASHING.

"Crashing."

CRASHING.   THE MOON IS MOVING TOWARD OUR POSITION AT A RATHER ASTONISHING RATE OF SPEED. I CALCULATE WE HAVE TEN MINUTES UNTIL IMPACT.

"Crashing on us?" Grond said. "How the fuck is it crashing on us?"

I HAVE NO IDEA, the *Nameless* responded. THE MOON ABRUPTLY DREW TO A STOP IN

THE SKY AND THEN JUST AS ABRUPTLY CHANGED DIRECTION AND BEGAN HURTLING TOWARD US. IT IS ACCELERATING.

"This elevator needs to go fucking faster," Grond said.

I HAVE ALREADY BEGUN TAKEOFF PROCEDURES, Namey said. PLEASE HURRY. THE MOON WILL OBLITERATE EVERYTHING FOR SEVERAL KILOMETERS IN EVERY DIRECTION WHEN IT IMPACTS THE PLANET. IT WOULD BE AN EXTINCTION-LEVEL EVENT WERE THERE ANY PREEXISTING LIFE ON THE PLANET.

"Shit. The miners." Brazel said. "See if you can get any communication with the settlement on the other side of this rock and let them know what's coming." *As if they'll believe it,* he thought. *Maybe if they made sure they were underground in time...*

I THOUGHT OF THAT ALREADY, Namey replied. I HAVE RECEIVED NO COMMUNICATION FROM THAT SETTLEMENT EITHER. I HAVE BEGUN RUNNING DIAGNOSTICS ON MY COMMUNICATIONS MODULES.

The two exchanged a look again. Had whatever happened to the research station happened on the other side of the planet as well?

A million years later, the lift finally slid into position on the top floor. Grond wasted no time, slamming the doors open. They fled for the front door.

Only to be stopped by the closed airlock door in the reception area.

"Oh, *fuck*," Grond said. He threw himself at the door, muscles straining, putting everything he had into shoving the door open. To no avail. The door was simply too big, even for him.

I ESTIMATE FIVE MINUTES, the *Nameless* said.

"Get your ass around to the back of the building!" Grond shouted. "There's a loading dock! Meet us outside! Fucking now!"

ON MY WAY.

Grond had much longer legs than Brazel, and was in much better shape than the gnome was. There was no time to wait for him, and no time to be polite about it. He snatched Brazel up from the ground and tucked him under one arm, running through the station at top speed back toward the loading dock, hoping he remembered the way. He saw the silhouette of the *Nameless* as it landed beyond the entryway, and sped out to the ship.

And then he looked up at the sky.

He had thought that the sight of one of Shithole's moons careening toward him would be the most terrifying thing he was going to see that day. It was not. The thing that had thrown the moon was.

He stood, jaws hanging open, until his partner punched him in the ribs.

"Go," Brazel choked. "Shockwave alone will kill us before it even hits. Keep running."

Grond tore his eyes away from the thing in the sky and sprinted toward the *Nameless*, which several feet off the ground, engines roaring, before he even reached it. He leapt for the hatch, hitting the floor and rolling, then bellowing for the ship to move as he spun back to his feet.

"What the fuck is that thing?" he said.

WHAT THING? Namey asked. Grond felt the ship accelerating under his feet.

"Just head the fuck away from the fucking moon!" he shouted, heading for his room. The cockpit was Brazel's, and sized for gnomes; Grond had a copilot's chair in his quarters that allowed him to see anything Brazel could see from the pilot's seat.

"What the fuck is that?" he said again.

He heard a strangled gasp from his partner and realized that Brazel was only now seeing the thing-- he'd been facing the ground in Grond's arms before they got aboard the ship.

The moon had been torn from space and thrown to the earth by the arms of an angry god.

It was immense; it *defied* immensity. Grond and Brazel had once encountered a deep-space teleporter that, for a brief moment, they'd mistaken for a moon. This dwarfed that object by an order of magnitude; it made the moon it had hurled look like a child's toy. It bore the faintest resemblance to a spidership; a central sphere, with dozens if not hundreds of tentacles extending from its equator. The tentacles themselves were composed of more connected spheres; Grond had the horrible feeling that if they were somehow severed from their parent, they would grow their own arms rather than die.

It hung in the sky, its arms moving, horribly alive and organic, synchronized and pulsating as if to a terrible celestial song that only it could hear.

The *Nameless* accelerated.

WE ARE AT SAFE DISTANCE, the ship reported.

"Not safe," Brazel mumbled crazily. "Never safe. Not from that. Keep going. Faster. Hit tunnelspace the second you fucking can." He'd never encountered or heard of anything living that could enter tunnelspace on its own. Could it still reach them? Those tentacles had to be dozens of kilometers long.

The moon crashed into the planet's surface, obliterating the mountain and everything beneath it, sending out a shockwave so great that it would circle the planet's surface three times before settling down. What little atmosphere 00901213 had burned. The ice sublimated, escaping the planet's gravity before refreezing in the cold of deep space. If there had been anything alive anywhere on the planet, underground or not, the earthquakes would have killed them by now.

The thing took no notice of them at all. It hung in the vacuum, watching the destruction it had wrought, and Brazel lost sight of it as his boat finally leapt into tunnelspace, heading home, heading to safety.

Neither of them spoke for a very long time.

⤐⟨⊙⟩⤏

THANK YOU

for reading *The Benevolence Archives, Vol. 1.*

If you enjoyed this book, please leave a review for it at the book review site of your choice.

ABOUT LUTHER M. SILER

Luther Siler was born in 1976. He lives in northern Indiana with his wife, three-year-old son, a dog and two cats. In his spare time he works at a middle school.

He only occasionally refers to himself in the third person, and writing this is making him slightly uncomfortable. He is also god-awful at smiling for pictures.

Luther Siler's blog:
        http://www.infinitefreetime.com

Follow Luther @nfinitefreetime on Twitter.

ALSO BY LUTHER M. SILER

The saga of the Benevolence Archives continues with

THE SANCTUM OF THE SPHERE: THE BENEVOLENCE ARCHIVES, VOLUME 2

"Go rob that train." Nice, normal. An everyday heist.

But nothing is ever normal for Brazel, Grond and Rhundi.

A simple act of motorized larceny quickly explodes into a galaxy-spanning adventure for the two thieves. Blade-wielding elves, a fast-moving global war, a secret outlaw space city, incomprehensible insectoids and one impossibly lucky human are just the start of their problems. And that's before they learn that someone from Grond's past has gotten the Benevolence involved...

What is happening on the ogrespace moon Khkk?

Who are the Noble Opposition?

And what is the secret of THE SANCTUM OF THE SPHERE?

Available digitally and in an omnibus print edition containing both volumes of THE BENEVOLENCE ARCHIVES.

SKYLIGHTS

Available in print and digitally.

August 15, 2022: the Tycho, the most advanced interplanetary craft ever designed by the human race, launches from Earth on an expedition to Mars. The Tycho carries four passengers, soon to be the most famous people in human history.

February 19, 2023: The Tycho loses all communication with Earth while orbiting Mars. After weeks of determined attempts to reestablish contact, the Tycho is declared lost.

2027: Journalist Gabriel Southern receives a message from a mysterious caller: "Mars." Ezekiel ben Zahav isn't talking, but he wants Southern to accompany him for something-- and he's dangling enough money under his nose to make any amount of hardship worth it.

SKYLIGHTS is the story of the second human expedition to Mars. Their mission: to find out what happened to the first.

Read on for an excerpt: the prologue to SKYLIGHTS.

Flashbulb memory, they call it. It's when you remember exactly where you were when you first discovered something or saw something happen.

If you're younger than me, which a lot of you probably are, then your first flashbulb memory is probably related to terrorism somehow. Anybody in, say, their early thirties or older probably remembers exactly where they were on September 11, 2001. A little younger than that and your first flashbulb memory is probably one of the bombings in Chicago in 2018.

I was six years old when the space shuttle *Challenger* exploded. It was January 29, 1986, at exactly eleven thirty-nine in the morning. I was in first grade. For some reason-- I could look this up if I wanted, I suppose, but my first-grade self didn't know, so I'm not going to bother-- NASA had decided that it would be great if they put a schoolteacher on the Space Shuttle. Her name was Christa McAuliffe, and she'd been a middle school teacher, her students not a lot older than I was at the time.

There was a ton of publicity about her presence on the shuttle. Come to think of it, that might have been the reason that NASA put her there in the first place. Every single kid in my school was watching the flight launch on television. The *Challenger* took off, and we all clapped. Seventy-three seconds later, an O-ring failed on the shuttle's right Solid Rocket Booster. There was a little puff of smoke from the side of the ship.

Some of us were still clapping.

I remember noticing it and wondering, for the split second that I had, what had happened. And then the *Challenger,* with me and millions of other people around the country watching, silently blew apart. There were a few seconds of shocked silence in the room, and then every kid in the class-- every one in the building, probably-- started crying at once.

You know what? Writing that just now, I wondered what my teacher must have done afterwards. I can't even remember her name. I can remember the wood surface on my desk, because I dug my fingers into it so hard that day that they scratched it and I got splinters. I can remember the wood-grain on the television set they had us watching. I can remember being surprised that Rachel Douglas, the biggest butthead in the entire first grade, was crying as hard as I was. But I can't remember a single thing that our teacher did to try and bring everybody back to sanity after watching that happen. That's how flashbulb memories work; you'll remember the event itself forever, but that doesn't mean you'll remember anything else that happened around it.

Seventeen years and two days later, it happened again. This time, it was the shuttle *Columbia*, and I was twenty-four and no longer sitting in a classroom. In fact, when the *Columbia* was falling apart in the morning sky over Texas, I was stuck in traffic and late to work. I found out about it about ten minutes after I got in, when the smarmy dope from the office next door made some sort of comment about it to me. We had the Internet by then-- yes, there was Internet back then, although I think we might have still been calling it the World Wide Web-- and I saw the entire thing on CNN's Web site. This time there weren't any tears, just a dull sort of ache in the pit of my stomach. I spent the rest of the day on the computer, chasing down eyewitness reports and trying to devour whatever little bits of actual news managed to leak out. It was funny; I hadn't spent much time thinking about space flight since the first grade, but suddenly the families of the men and women on that shuttle were all I could think about.

I was working for the *Indianapolis Star* at the time, splitting my time between a biweekly column in the science section and general reporting on local news for the rest of the paper. It was a good job; I was happy enough, and making enough money, but I wanted something different from my life.

I decided to write a book.

A year later, I'd completed *Nothing to Bury: the Martyrs of the Space Race*, a look at the lives of the astronauts who had died on the *Challenger* and the *Columbia*, as well as a host of other lives lost in the pursuit of space, and a look at the culture of NASA in between the two disasters. I was pretty proud of it as a piece of work; I wasn't expecting it to necessarily sell well to the general public, but it was a good piece of writing. It did better than I'd expected, enough that I've been able to be comfortable with freelance writing since then. I'm still working for news sites and some of the few print papers that are left, mind you, but I can pick my own assignments and do my own reporting now as opposed to having people assign my projects.

You know where this is going, don't you? I imagine you do.

On August 15, 2022, after years of technical and political delays, the space shuttle *Tycho*, carrying four astronauts, launched on a six-month journey to Mars. They were to remain in orbit around Mars for thirty days, during which they would land on the planet's surface for the first time in human history, then to return to Earth. The run-up to the launch was the biggest public relations bonanza NASA had ever seen. Everything just *stopped* the day the *Tycho* launched. It was just like it had been for the *Challenger,* only times a hundred. They just weren't as good at hype in the eighties, I guess.

I was watching at home, with a couple of friends-- I actually had a little party for the launch. I didn't realize how tense I was until I looked at my hands afterwards. There were furrows in my palms from my fingernails. Then the shuttle took off, soaring into a perfectly blue sky, and I held my breath for a few moments.

The launch went off without a hitch, though, and pictures of the *Tycho* blanketed every website and print doc on the planet over the next few days. For the next six months, everyone was obsessed with Mars. The astronauts provided regular updates on what they were doing. You could get daily blink messages from them if you wanted to, and progress along their flight path was updated live on a map running at the top of CNN.com for the entire duration of the trip. Those six months, I'm convinced, inspired a whole generation of new astronauts, astrophysicists, and pilots. I've never in my life seen America more excited about science. It was amazing.

And then, on February 19th, 2023, when the long voyage was finally over, we... well, we don't actually know what happened. The *Tycho* was supposed to aerobrake into orbit around Mars, stay in orbit for a day or two, and then the astronauts were going to leave the ship to descend to the planet's surface in a lander. They were going to stay on the surface for two weeks or so, doing experiments, exploring the Martian surface, and making history.

There wasn't anything resembling photo evidence, not good evidence at least-- NASA had been sending a steady diet of pictures and video from cameras affixed to the outside of the *Tycho* for months, but they failed at the same time as the audio feed. But we were getting audio beamed back from inside the cabin. Right up until the point where the flight commander, a decorated Marine pilot by the name of Alondra Gallegos, spoke the last words that the *Tycho* sent back to Earth.

"Is that..." was all she said.

After that, nothing. No sound, no signals, no big explosion to be played on the news over and over again. Just nothing at all, and what started off as mild concern slowly morphed, over the next few days, weeks, months, into the certainty that, somehow, the ship had been lost. There was hope for a while that there had just been some sort of global communications failure, that the *Tycho* was still out there but had lost the ability to talk to us. Sadly, those hopes didn't make much sense in reality-- the *Tycho's* communication capabilities were among the simplest systems on the ship, something a talented twelve-year-old would have been able to repair, *and* there was a redundant backup system. Anything catastrophic enough to have completely crippled the ship's ability to talk would have caused fatal damage to the rest of the ship as well. We just couldn't figure out what. Conventional wisdom eventually decided there had been some sort of asteroid or meteorite impact, something like that.

There was no flashbulb moment for the *Tycho*. The families of the four people lost on that mission-- Alondra Gallegos, Harrison Brown, Kassius Newsome, and Ai-Li Wu-- will never be able to move on. Many of them are convinced that their family members are still out there somewhere. There was no national mourning like there was for the *Challenger* and the *Columbia*. It was as if, after three high-profile ship losses, this time the country just wanted to forget about it.

I got a few calls for interviews after the *Tycho* lost contact, and a few more a few months later, once NASA officially stopped trying to reestablish contact with the ship. I turned them all down, though; I didn't want to base any more of my career on profiting from the deaths of people more heroic and important than I was. I didn't want to write about space any more.

Little did I know.